C.R. Couron knows how to open a story. The novel *Reality?* opens with a gripping depiction of the character Yolanda running for her life. Couron's prose captures with descriptive power the sheer terror and physical sensation Yolanda experiences attempting to save her life. It sucks a reader into the novel's fictional world.

The novel unfolds in a series of quasi-vignettes and set pieces. This narrative structure, however, never dulls the book's sharp kaleidoscopic edge. An important reason why is Couron develops each section in complete fashion rather than short-cutting the reader in some way. It is impressive the amount of plot Couron packs into a brief novel yet resolves each aspect of the story by the end. Some readers may complain of over-plotting depending on personal preference.

Couron powers the story with physical and confident prose. The gripping talent for depicting action and pointed dialogue further fuel the story. Judge a novel's value by its genre. Judging a speculative or even a suspense novel by the standards of a literary novel is asinine.

Another strength of the book is its hard-charging pace. Couron cuts any potential fat off the narrative and steams ahead. The author can do this because it's clear after finishing *Reality?* Couron began writing with total clarity about how to tell this tale. There are no missteps. Nothing is tentative.

There is literary merit in this book as well. Couron questions readers about the question behind the title in an artful way without ever transforming the narrative into some philosophical broadside disguised as fiction. Enlarging the novel's thematic spectrum elevates its overall impact on the reader. Few demands writers in this fictional area to investigate larger concerns, even on the sly, but Couron deserves credit for it.

Readers will enjoy its short length. *Reality?* demands little of your time but engages you without any lulls. This is crucial. Mixing the headlong energy of popular fiction with top drawer writing and artistic sophistication sets this book apart. The same focus defining the novel serves the conclusion as well and it is a great payoff to the preceding story.

The final verdict, in the end, is if a writer holds your attention and Couron does that. How it's done is immaterial. Couron makes you care about the people in this story and imbues each with the mark of human nature. They are never cardboard cutouts and we are swept along by their pursuits and passions.

Uncertain times like this call for entertaining storytellers capable of distracting us. C.R. Couron's *Reality?* fits the bill without striking a heavy-handed note. It never wastes reader's time and maintains a level of readability inviting anyone to travel through its pages. These sort of books never go out of style.

- Jason Hillenburg, Reprospace Reviews™

REALITY?

C.R. COURON

Reality?
First edition, published 2020

By C.R. COURON
Copyright © 2020, C.R. COURON

Cover design by Reprospace.com

Paperback ISBN-13: 978-1-952685-12-5

Published by Kitsap Publishing
Poulsbo, WA 98370
www.KitsapPublishing.com

A Collection of Adventures

I really hope you enjoy my first book in The *Reality?* Series. Please be on the look out for *What Reality?* and *Is this Reality?* coming soon.

Acknowledgments

To the incredible Lady that is my Soulmate and Wife that has endured loney hours, reading and rereading manuscripts and supporting my desire to write. I thank her with all my heart.

PART ONE

CHAPTER ONE

Yolanda

The sounds of guns firing, people screaming, and the roaring of bull horns began receding into the background. Heart pounding, breath burning, and feet racing had become her entire world. Chest and feet felt like they were on fire, yet her legs felt numb. There was an opening. She would escape, then something slammed into her, spinning, so that she faced where she had come from. Tear gas canisters were exploding everywhere. Pain erupted when one of the tear gas canisters struck her shoulder. Panic exploded, renewing her ability to move her legs.

"Run, run," she screamed, not knowing if the words were coming from her mouth or her mind. The next explosion was in her head. Then blackness.

"Yolanda! Yolanda Swiftriver! Can you hear me?" Someone was shouting. She didn't care. It was still dark. She drifted back into the blackness.

Today, yesterday and all the past fled to the darkness. Swimming to the light, laying by a river, cold, cold, cold. Darkness flooded her mind. Falling, floating, scared, lost.

Dreams or visions of screaming people, dark angry men and sounds of gunfire near and far. Fear flooded her mind. Horses and cars, warriors of her tribe, cops and soldiers, a time far in the past, as if it happened only yesterday. This was Yolanda's reality as she lay in the hospital bed. Neither the woman trapped in the bed nor the doctor standing by her bed knew if one day she would open her eyes and return to reality.

CHAPTER TWO

DEAN

Wobbling back and forth, the Navy Attack Bomber shuddered and bounced. The airplane and its three-person crew were in the turbulent air currents boiling behind the aircraft carrier lying dead ahead. Safety harnesses cinched tight, holding them in their seat pan. The pilot fighting to keep the aircraft on the bright light called the meatball, flashing red, then green, then red, and finally a steady green as the light guided them to the carrier's steel flight deck. At the sametime the flight deck continued bobbing up and down appearing it was fighting to avoid them. As the aircraft came closer, the flight deck dropped, then rose and rolled with the sea as if it was a dance that only it knew. The plane screamed towards it, bouncing and twisting as if it was alive and the pilot assessed the rhythm of the carrier's flight deck.

Just as it seemed the powerful aircraft would crash, the pilot heard "Cut, Cut, Cut," a command for him to cut power to the monster twin jet engines. Screaming engines began quieting as the double throttles were slid to idle. Pilot and crew slammed hard into the aircraft's seat pans, microseconds before throttles were slammed again to a hundred percent engine power, in case the airplane's tail hook missed the arresting wire. Engines screamed back to full power just as the crew was thrown forward hard into their shoulder harnesses.

The plane's pointed nose slammed down hard toward the deck, as it came to a violent stop, once the tail hook caught the wire. Throttles were pulled back to idle, engines once again winding down to a mild whine as the nose came back up. The massive cable, called the wire, dropped from the bomber's tail hook. The dance had successfully been completed they had made another safe landing.

The acrid smell of J.P. 5 jet fuel, burnt rubber, oil, and jet blast flooded the cockpit as third crewman Paul Simpson unstrapped from his parachute and shoulder straps. Sliding off the seat into a crouch until he was able to unlatch and pop open the upper hatch of the cockpit. Dean "Thunder" Hawkins, the pilot, had a flashing memory of how this man had changed everything when not returning to the ship after a night of liberty.

In the next few days, he would be saying goodbye to this man. Dean had sworn to himself to never use the nickname he and Jack "Eyes" Eiman, his navigator/bombardier, had hung on this man named Paul.

That was back when the three of them were drinking in a bar outside Cubic Point, Philippines. Dean and Eyes decided to take the new crewman to town and initiate him into the flight crew. It was not long before the three of them were in an alcohol buzz. With a slurring drunk tongue, "Eyes" started staring at Paul and then started to chuckle. The chuckle built into roaring laughter. Tears were running down his cheeks when Eyes pointed at Paul. Between sobbing laughs sputtered, "Your damn nose nostrils look like the twin engines of a F-4 fighter's jet intakes,"

Paul, looking confused, replied,

"Pardon me, but I really think you've had too much to drink. Proof positive when you think a nose can look like a jet engine?" At that moment, Thunder also began to laugh. Paul still didn't get it and stood up and made his way toward the restroom.

They laughed even harder when Paul returned and asked if they were talking about the size of his nostrils . The name stuck, and it wasn't until many months later that Dean decided Paul had been unaware that was the day his flight crew had accepted him as one of them. Now long after that, Dean understood it was really the day Paul thought because of his color he was just someone that happened to be in their flight crew, not someone they respected.

Dean was just tired. At times, he felt like a punch drunk fighter who kept trying to win, yet time and again ended face-first. Years ago, he had a plan, get a college degree with a major in psychology. He wanted to learn what made people do what they did and believe things that made no sense truthfully, he had to accept that one of those people was a man named Dean.

Now he had over fifty successful missions completed by arriving back to what they called the nest in one piece. Slamming onto the deck, throttles at a hundred percent, engines screaming and everything about the airplane trying to claw its way back into the sky. Adrenalin flooding, panic, and or frozen fear, trying to take his mind and body. This mixed with the pure joy of flying all the while fighting for another wire to catch and one more safe landing. He and his crew all knew it would always take a while before the adrenalin flood would dissipate and drop them into a canyon of exhaustion.

Thinking this was it, the end of his third tour in far east Asia, this one lasting more than seven months. The third deployment of never-ending bombing this small country, Thunder knew little of besides a mission briefing and then the next catapult shot. Twenty-four hours a day for weeks on end, bombing, landing, sleeping, and then starting the cycle all over. Unlike Eyes and the man once called "Intake," this was his last cruise, and that was that. Thunder was returning to the States, a place he and most others were calling the world. Three journeys to far east Asia specifically to protect the southern part of Vietnam from the North Vietnamese and Cambodian incursions that were invading them was enough, Thunder was done! He would soon just be Dean, not the man nicknamed Thunder. He was really done this time.

After debriefing, Thunder would begin the tedious process of checking out of his squadron. Next, he would start the goodbyes with his shipmates, crew members, and attempt to find a way to apologize for degrading Paul, the man he had once helped "Eyes" nickname Intake. While stripping off his uniform and titles of a well-decorated Navy pilot, he wondered what his identity would revert to? One thing he was sure of, was the future status of Dean Hawkins was not known.

The first time he had returned to the states, it wasn't long before fear and confusion replaced the joy of being back. His country had changed; it had become a different reality. People were tearing apart cities, schools, and families. He was leaving a war that wasn't called one, just to return home to another type of war that could not, should not be happening.

For the first time, he had felt glad he lacked a family to face and maybe tear apart. The fabric of what he considered a home or whatever he would be calling the USA seemed to be exploding in violence and anger. It was slicing through the fabric of relationships both in families and on the streets of America. Three times he had found ways to justify and believe he was participating in a just war. Both times returning home, he saw more of his generation protesting and hating what he and the rest of the military forces were doing to Southeast Asia.

All this seemed to increase his need to justify what he believed was his duty. On this last cruise, he began accepting that maybe he was here to understand his place in the issues surrounding the war, including the societal changes taking place at home.

Most of the time, he was just too tired and numb to care. There were even times when anger was all he could feel. None of these things made the war more bearable or understandable. Each new ship faded into the last, and each mission was part of the previous. Even the countries with their exotic cities became one.

Then all hell exploded and it was not the war he was fighting. Nor the war he knew was taking place back in the states. This war was here and now, between shipmates, and brought home the hardest when Paul "Intake" Simpson had not returned to the ship from liberty. It was the last time it was moored in the Philippines. Now that man, Paul, was sitting in the seat across from him.

The thunder of the engines, catapult officer signaling, and Dean saluting that he was ready, all overtook his ability to continue thinking, as his body was being slammed by the incredible G-force of the catapult. The catapult increased the massive plane's acceleration to launch speed in a little more than four seconds. Its forces rippling as the A3D's fuselage skin absorbed the building G-forces that kept pressing him harder and harder into the seat.

The thundering of the aircraft's engines subsided as they left the flight deck. The plane began to gently drop before its wings grabbed air and started to climb. Both he and Paul, once called "Intake," let out a breath and settled into the flight, taking them to Hawaii.

Paul was the only crew flying with him and was sitting second seat, where Eyes usually sat. Paul would stay in Hawaii to await transportation to another Carrier headed for Yankee Station. Dean, instead, would be boarding a civilian airliner back to the States.

Once they climbed to altitude and set the craft's heading for the Philippines, Dean relaxed and thought about this last flight in an aircraft he had hated. Initially, like most in flight school training, he wanted to fly Fighters. Instead, he was ordered to these aircraft, the largest onboard any aircraft carriers. A plane referred to as the "Whale" by flight deck crews and others. The official designation for them was A3D Skywarriors. Some people even suggested that the A3D stood for all three dead as they tended to kill their crews when attempting to bail out before crashing. Now on this last time flying the big bird, he had to admit he would miss the big whale.

Now it was time to say goodbye to the whale and think about returning to the States; the only thing between him and all the craziness he had left in the States was his final physical and discharge. What was genuinely unknown to him was what he would do when he received his last paycheck, he guessed that would be anybody's bet. Hopefully, the trip back would give him plenty of time to sort out the pieces after apologizing to Paul.

One night Paul had not returned from liberty in Olongapo outside of Naval Air Station, Cubi Point in the Philippines. This initiated a change in Dean's ignorance of civil-rights as practiced in the United States. Dean seldom left the base to visit Olongapo, a town right outside the Main Gate; instead, he spent most of his free time in the Officer's Club or aboard the Ship. Paul was an enlisted aircrew man and Enlisted men and Officers seldom spent time together on liberty and enlisted were not authorized in the Officer's Club. This tended to help keep Dean naive and isolated to the segregation practiced in the Navy. What happened to Paul and shattered Dean's naive' was only a month ago. Now at 12 thousand feet as the plane was basically flying itself, he looked over at Paul while asking,

"What the hell happened?" When all he got was a stare and a shrug, Dean qualified his question, "You know the riot and all that?"

After a long silence, Paul began to talk, first with a lot of what seemed caution, then with increased underlying anger. He began describing returning to the squadron and being placed under investigation. They said he participated in what they referred to as a race riot. It happened the same night a friend of his was beaten to death. Paul had not been aware of it but was just trying to return to the Ship. He and five of his friends attempted to board one of the cattle cars.

Paul paused for a moment seeing the confused expression flood over Dean's face and said, "You know the moving van type of truck with benches attached to the outer walls. They take the place of buses for carrying us enlisted sailors back to the Ship. That night instead of us and my friends being allowed to climb in, we were pushed off and told, (Your kind aren't allowed!) The white sailors began to laugh when one of my friends with me re-attempted to board,

"Keep trying," one of the Whites in the cattle car said,

"And you might die just like another one of you jungle bunnies did earlier tonight."

"It took us almost two hours to get back to the ship," Paul continued by saying,

"When we finally made it back, a brawl had broken out on the hanger deck there must have been near a hundred sailors involved. All of us Blacks in or around the area were arrested along with just very few Whites. The white guys had to outnumbered us 20 to 2. Seven of us Black men were cuffed and taken to the brig. For the White guys, there were only two." When Dean asked what had happened to get the Black man killed. Paul replied,

"I guess he didn't agree to only being allowed to go to the area of town called the "Jungle," but not allowed in the White area of Olongapo." I was not aware of this and told Paul so,

"Well, even in the enlisted club on base, we are expected to, as they say, stay with our own kind," he said, using quotation marks in the air in an angry gesture.

Then he continued describing what else had happened in the enlisted club, cattle car, in town and how it continued onto the ship. Paul's statements made it quite clear why he was not at the morning muster the day after all this happened.

Dean remembered sitting down for dinner where Eyes, the navigator/bombardier, was seated the day after the hanger bay riot. How he was stunned when Eyes began summarizing the hanger bay incident saying,

"Can you believe what those drunken bunch of Nig,"

Dean cut his tirade off saying,

"Are you suggesting that Paul had a part in starting that riot?"

"Absolutely! What other reason did the Skipper have for pulling him from flight status?"

It took Dean a moment to connect that Eyes was talking about Paul, someone they had been flying with for almost seven months. Dean had been unaware Paul was pulled from flight status because he was accused of being in the hanger deck brawl.

He began to review how he had minimized what Paul had told him earlier that day. When he was released from the brig and returned to the squadron, Paul caught up with him while Dean was running laps. As he ran beside him, Paul said he had been attacked because he was Black and then accused of starting a fight. Dean remembered thinking Paul was just trying to downplay his part in the incident. That is until Eyes stood in front of Dean, and included Paul, by saying, "As one of those kinds of drunken damn," Dean once more cut him off when Paul began to use the same words as before. The sad part is the man standing in front of him, was unable to connect, that Dean had cut him off twice for the same reason.

To resolve some of his confusion, Dean pulled Paul's service records for a review. He discovered five things he had never paid attention to when Paul became part of the flight crew;

Paul's evaluations throughout his six-year career were never lower than a 3.9 out of 4.0,

His advancement was granted each time he was eligible,

His advancement test scores in every cycle were in the top ten percentile,

His training evaluations and test scores for A3D third crewman training were 4.0, and his training school scores were in the top five percentile,

He agreed to reenlist contingent on flight training and third crewman status.

Dean also focused on investigating further into the matter that led to Paul sitting across from him in the cockpit inbound to Pearl Harbor, Hawaii. That had been the first time Dean began to realize the degree of segregation and bigotry happening all around him. He heard these words used before this, he somehow had not heard them. He also began to see behaviors that he had not noticed before in his fellow shipmates.

These revelations came to life when his Commanding Officer revoked Paul's flight status, thus deactivating his third crewman credentials. Paul's dreams had been tossed in the trash. The additional salt in his wounds was that Paul was still required to complete the rest of his enlistment. An enlistment he had been required to sign prior to third crewman flight training.

The last time Dean spoke with Paul was after they debriefed from their flight to Hawaii. Dean had looked into the man's eyes and acknowledged how the nickname "Intake" was an implied racial slur, and how he had not heard what Paul had been attempting to say in relation to it. Nor had he understand how deeply Paul could be and was hurt by Dean, basically blowing off how hurt and disrespected Paul was because of having a dark complexion.

This man was just as important a crew member as himself and Eyes when they manned their combat aircraft. In one way or another, all their lives depended on each other, from the moment they began the preflight checklist of the plane until they debriefed after the mission. Dean was not sure if Paul knew how deeply Dean felt, but he did remember tears forming in Paul's eyes as they shook hands, briefly hugged, and said goodbye. Dean would never forget how Paul stood up, walked over to Dean, and man-to-man thanked him for attempting to understand something he said that he thought Dean might never understand. At that moment, Dean believed he might never be as strong and righteous as the man who just shook his hand.

After participating in over four years of this war, Dean felt much more confused than when he initially joined the Navy. He had wanted to serve his country and, yes, escape from the pain of breaking up with Yolanda, but he never suspected he would need to apologize to Paul for all that Dean had not known and understood. Nor for what Dean had seen and learned about what they were doing in Nam. Or what he had heard and learned about what was going on in the States. A real brain freeze was building behind his eyes. He had thought he was serving a noble purpose, now all that and more had shattered. Now he had little or no understanding of what the HELL was going on!

Even during the flights that took him from the ship to the Philippines and then to Hawaii, his frustration in looking for answers continued to grow. While participating in a discharge physical, the impact of resigning from his Navy Commission began adding to all the other unanswered questions. Boarding a Tiger Airlines for his flight to the States left him little time for distraction. His confusion and future planning just kept growing more complex, yet with no resolution. He finally just tried to settle back in his seat. He attempted to get comfortable but continued feeling very uncomfortable in the airliner's body, not in the cockpit, not in control, just at the mercy of someone else at the flight controls. For at least an hour, he fidgeted, unable to get comfortable and nap. His mind spinning in and out of all he had been through and left behind. About the country, he had been bombing and the country he was returning too.

Even with all these thoughts running laps in his mind, Yolanda kept coming to the forefront. He met her while working on his Bachelor's Degree. A woman that embodied pretty much everything he was not interested in. The closest description of her would be "an outspoken sociology major." Plus, she, is or at least was, a Democrat, and even worse, she had embraced the so-called hippy groups. But by God, there was something about her, or maybe within her, that made her seem incredible.

Not until he met Paul was there any understanding of what Yolanda believed. Dean could not understand from the first day he had spent with her, but something deep in his soul must-have. A belief based on something he had never admitted to anybody. That he actually signed up for a class on witchcraft just because she had signed up for it. The crazy part was he did it even before they had officially met.

He was still unable to explain what happened. He just fell in love, head over heels type of falling in love. Then Viet Nam happened.

Yolanda joined rallies and demonstrations at first because of how deeply she belived in equal rights. Dean was hesitant to participate because he did not openly agree with the causes she stood for. He did not join the marches and rallies protesting for civil rights or against what was happening in Far East Asia. He was just not that type of guy.

When she started to march openly and rally against her own country and not standing up against the Communist trying to take over Viet Nam, it was too big a pill to swallow. She was a real damn dove. Instead of backing our rights and supporting our government, she began marching against those she called "Hawks." Then she started scolding him for being one. So his pride and honor pushed his decision to join the United States Navy, and to be honest, anger was the energizer. Now six years later, he knew how wrong he was.

The first wrong was the issue of civil rights. Dean was wrong, wrong, wrong because she dared to stand up and be counted while he just sat in the background. The worst part was when he finally began to understand how his ignorance had fed right into what was happening. He just did not know what it was like to have a different color of skin.

This, along with so many more memories, questions, and regrets, took his mind hostage. He could not sleep, found no joy, and definitely no peace. After what had seemed like an eternity, he was finally watching California's shoreline turning into land passing under the airplane.

All the travel hours melted as the enormous airliner's tires chirped on U.S, pavement as they were landing at Travis Air force Base. Looking out the window he felt like he was arriving in a foreign country.

CHAPTER THREE

Dances-as-Rain

An updraft pushed up on her as she spread her wings, embracing the air pressure and rising. Each spiral moved her higher. As she climbed higher, she saw flames licking upwards and felt the heavens becoming closer. The sounds of chanting men, first faintly, then becoming increasing more robust as she soared higher, and enticing her to come closer.

She knew it was forbidden to be present at the male gathering, but she did not veer from where the drum's deep sounds began to pulsate against her, then within her body. Singing voices caressed and entwined with each heartbeat of drums. The music called, pulled, and stroked. The songs were a plea to the Creator,

May Your Power, balance our fear!
May Your Strength, balance our weakness!
May Your Wisdom, balance our ignorance!

Each verse pulled harder at her spirit. The wind beneath her wings offered the strength to rise toward the mountain's crown. The song demanded that she land.

Yolanda knew this must be a dream. The words were not in any language she knew, yet she understood this strange language without trying. It was as if she was an observer within a dream, observing. The way they spoke in this place, in this dream, was beautiful and musical. Each word had deep meaning and was made up of underlying melodies within the lyrics of the songs drumming.

Without knowing how, she knew names were sacred and not shared lightly. Only the medicine woman, her mother, and someday possibly her mate would know her name. The only other creature who would share this sacred word would be her spirit-helper.

The knowledge flooded her like the hug of a mother. Owl is her spirit helper! She is one with Owl as they fly above the earth, floating up along the mountainside, slowly rising to the sacred meeting place of the male elders. Owl's name, *Seer-in-the-Dark*, is a knowing thing for Dances-as-Rain. She did not know how she knew these things she just did.

Her sacred name is *"Dances-as-Rain"*. During the Naming ceremony, her feet danced as raindrops, touching the ground and bouncing back up. She had felt one with the rain. The rain fell so gladly from the clouds, then changed its mind for just a split moment when it hit the earth. It was as if each drop had a fear of becoming one with the ground. Instead, they seemed to reach back up to the sky and clouds. Then each touched back down and became part of the land. It was the rhythm, the rain danced, and she stepped into the rhythm and became one with the raindrops.

Now Owl was calling, showing Dances-as-Rain her clan's male spiritual leaders, the Elders and Medicine Men. They were all gathered high on *sacred mountain* so as to be closer to *Grandfather Creator* who lives above the sky. She knew not how she knew, yet she knew they were asking *Grandfather Creator* about the changing.

She knew Owl was her spirt helper, and she must find a Medicine Woman to lead her to awareness. Only then would there be understanding of dreams, and precisely this dream!

Female spirit leaders were beginning to gather in *Mother Forest*, closer to *Grandmother Life-Giver* who lived within the earth. The mountain top was not where she belonged, the power of the female's song pulled at her spirit until she knew her place was in the forest.

With a mighty shudder, Owl released its mighty wings laying

them tightly against its side: Owl turned and dove back toward Mother Earth.

At that moment, a chant filled Dances-as-Rain's mind;

"Grandfather provides materials,

for life

Grandmother nourishes

these materials into life."

Owl then silently glided to a branch and perched above the woman gathering. Dances-as-Rain staring through the eyes of Owl observes the gathering. She is flooded with awareness of her people's connections and heritage. They are her people, they are who she is!

The dance of *Tells-Stories* is the history of creation. How *Grandfather-Spirit Giver* gave the people a spirit that thirsts for balance. Balance is the way of honor. That is why there are the spirits of good and evil. The Creator first created balance. But balance always includes conflicts such as good and evil, so Creator made all things unbalanced; thus, the spirits would always strive toward balance instead of unbalancing;

The sky needs the earth,

the ground needs the air,

how else could the people live.

The people are guardians of all the life brought by the rain, the air we breathe, and the water we drink.

The threads of life must dance within the tapestry.

The tapestry must have air between the threads;

otherwise,

how would we weave the tapestry?

Water comes from the lakes, rivers, and seas.

then rises to the sky;

otherwise,

how would we fill the thirst

of all that is of the earth?

How do the threads weave the tapestry?

If not for the plants that need the water,

falling from the sky?

How do we send the seeds and the pollen that makes new life if not for the wind, rain, sun, and moon?

All these and so much more

cannot be counted

as they bring

all we are and all we will be.

This and more Dances-as-Rain hears and sees. Sitting on a branch in a tree, that grows from the earth and reaches to the sky. Receiving the sun, rain, and wind, so it will grow and spread across the land. The fire flickers and the people dance as Dances-as-Rain cries with joy for she is home and with her people.

She now knows that her mother's people are directly connected to the *As-One clan*, which is said to be one with the animals. Her father's people are connected to the *Wind-Whistler* clan that understands the language of the wind. The people are made up of nine tribes, each having nine clans, and each clan is comprised of three groups of three families.

She knows that Yolanda Swiftriver is not her. Her sacred name is *Dances-as-Rain*. The Owl is her spirit helper, and its name is *Seer-in-the-Dark*, and the people are the *Walk-a-la, she* knows Yolanda Swiftriver is not her sacred name, Dances-as-Rain. Owl is spirit helper, Owls name is *Seer-in-the-Dark*, people are the *Walk-a-la*, she knows her name, she knows her,,, she knows,, she…

CHAPTER FOUR

Professor Damon Soule

Marigold University

Dr. Damon Soule, a trim athletic man, checked the restroom mirror as he dried his hands on the obnoxious paper towels. White bushy eyebrows. Black thick hair, slicked back, turning white at the temples, with an exaggerated widow's peak and a sharply trimmed black goatee coming to an excellent point. The overall look was finished by a matching center triangle of white in the middle of the goatee. With a satisfied smile in what he saw looking back at him, he finished drying his hands.

Damon almost believed Marigold U and every other place of knowledge had been built around white chipped enamel containers that reluctantly gave up paper towels. Paper towels containing the essence of fingernails scraping on blackboards. He never understood how a University awarding Ph.D.'s in psychology could use, or worse yet, purchase such a product. One that has only one purpose in life, which was to irritate, then fall apart before anyone could dry their hands. It would be no wonder if the person inventing paper towels had also chuckled when they were placed in a room referred to as a restroom. Even when Damon was not on edge, he hated the damn things.

Today is the first class of this year and even after teaching for years, each new school year felt new. He took immense pride in being a favorite professor in his department. His classes were always on the first-to-fill-list. He was sure both his appearance and controversial research were the initial attractors. He also believed that his teaching style and abilities brought students back for additional courses. A controversial piece of this style was being one of the very few Professors encouraging his students to call him by his first name. He believed it would stimulate a more active classroom environment. He soon he became known as Dr. D.

A new school year was beginning it was a warm and beautiful September. He thought about returning to his office for one final review of his notes. Changed his mind knowing for this class he didn't need cheat sheets because it was a class that had been a pivotal point in both his career and research. It never seemed to get old, even after teaching it all these years. The students seemed to love the class as much as he loved teaching it.

With one last look in the mirror, his beard pointed, hair slicked back and bushing his eyebrows up a bit, he left the so-called restroom. Yolanda was on his mind. Since Dean joined the Navy and left for Vietnam, she hadn't been the same. Thinking about her and Dean reminded him of the first time he offered this class. It had taken one hell of a battle to get departmental approval to teach it. Any course titled *Witchcraft/Shamanism, a Psychological and Sociological Approach*, was bound to raise some eyebrows.

The primary hurdle initiated against the class's approval was from none other than the colleague he thought of as "the Walrus." The man even sported a thick white-whiskered Fu Manchu type of mustache that Damon thought resembled two huge tusks. Their first introduction was at the Fall pre-semester department meeting. Both were freshly hired assistant professors to the Social Science department. Professor Swintnt's hire proceeded Damon's by maybe three months. They both knew the other was competing for a job each semester, thus also knew they were competitors for advancement to associate professor. That alone pitted them against one another.

Damon and Dr. Byron Swintnt came to a mutual agreement to disagree the first time they had shook hands. In ten years of association, that original agreement had yet to be compromised.

By the end of their third year, both had completed and published research. This provided advancement for both to the level of associate professorships. During this time, their feud had not only continued; it had escalated into underlying all-out warfare. Fuel for the fire was further added by Dr. Swintnt's and Damon's research being of very different natures, yet belonging in a related field.

CHAPTER FIVE

Professor Byron Swintnt

Professor Byron Swintnt had just received the proposed class schedule for the fall semester. First, he reviewed the plan concerning his classes, and as usual, he studied everyone else's in the department. It was one way to judge the amount of respect the Department Head gave him. Being an Associate Professor, the title alone deserved to be respected; besides, the assigned classes tended to identify how the Professor was regarded.

Scanning the list of assigned classes he would be able to make comparisons based on how he has placed, vis a'vis someone such as Damon Soule. He and Soule were both Associate Professors, yet he had almost three months seniority over him. That alone rated one less 200 level class with a possibility of one more 300 level class than Soule.

"Damn, I hate that man's name, no one, and I do mean no one! should have a name such as Soule. Really! Like he has a soul. Students understand, as most do not refer to him as Dr. Soule. Instead, they refer to him as Dr. D. He acts as if the students respect him. That is not a sign of respect, why it, is an insult. He is a University Professor for Heaven's sake, not somebody's chum!"

Making chuckling noises, he returned to studying the class listing. The chuckling was changed to a choking, then to coughing, then sputtering when he saw a course titled *Witchcraft/Shamanism, a Psychological and Sociological Approach 342.* He managed to catch his breath. Then just quit breathing altogether, finally exhaled loudly, stood up, did not bother to close his office door and stormed down the Hall toward the classroom belonging to Damon Soule. The department's golden boy, Chancellor Folks had approved it!

When Damon had first presented that ridiculous idea, maybe two weeks ago, yes, that was it, at the pre-semester staff meeting, he had total faith, the idea would not be accepted. Talk around the table suggested otherwise as several professors displayed interest, even support of the proposal. His opinion, on the other hand, was met with polite acceptance for his input. Then the Chancellor had adjourned the meeting and left the room.

Professor Swintnt's insides and even his intellect was screaming in opposition. He began to feel close to getting physical. Instead, with face turning red, he had stood up and waddled from the room, his massive hindquarters quivering with each angry step. Storming down the hallway passed Damon's office while glaring, and saying, "We will see. That so-called Professor better understand that we will see… just you wait and see!" Then he continued muttering the same words. Finally found himself struggling to find more words that would show his displeasure with Mister Damon Soule. This had to be the first time, at least, the first time he could remember having a problem like this. Nevertheless, just the idea of someone like Damon having the gall to think up a class like that was just too much.

Professor Swintnt had to admit he was embarrassed when leaving the staff meeting after Soule proposed that imbecilic class. In the hall he had raised his voice, letting Soule observe him losing his composure. Behavior that he knew must have been suggestive that he was near experiencing a catatonic seizure. It had just made him look like a fool. For heaven's sake, he hoped no one else was in viewing and or hearing distance. Even if Damon reported his outburst, no one would believe it was anything more than a difference of opinions.

Continuing his internal rage, he thought, "I earned my Associate

Professorship on my original research! Research Professor Wescoat was so impressed that he forwarded it to a respected *British Journal of Parapsychology*. The Journal referred to it as a significant shift toward experimental methodology and academic discipline. Not only THAT, it was also an acknowledged contribution to the field. It is prime time to recognize the field of precognition as a legitimate behavioral area of study. It is also time to end the controversy and begin a legitimate scientific study of these extrasensory abilities."

Dr. Wescoat, when he was the Assistant Dean of the Psychology Department, was an advocate of adding curriculum that would bring the University and himself recognition by the academic world. He encouraged my research in order to present a scientific-based experimental model for understanding Parapsychology. Contrary to Damon Soule's opinion; I propose to prove he is the one running around chasing a ludicrous belief that it is possible to experience pre-birth experiences. Now how ridiculous is that!

In the near future, I will be introducing psionic, a new discipline for applying principles of engineering utilizing electronics to the study of the paranormal and also psychic phenomenon, such as telepathy and psychokinesis. It will, by God, revolutionize the study of these misunderstood areas of human abilities. I believe this will be the breakthrough for scientific analysis bringing credibility to these areas of research at last!

Nevertheless, according to that know-it-all, damnable Damon, the research was flawed and of little relevance. At the same time, he thinks his own endeavors are brilliant and of significance to the field of psychology. Why he even openly ridiculed this research of mine... as a bunch of card tricks. The final nail in Soule's lack of understanding was when he did not understand the use of the Greek letter ψ pronounced as PSI generally used to denote the psychic functions of telepathy, clairvoyance, precognition psychokinesis, and extrasensory perception.

My research subjects were able to show over a ten percent probability in positive extrasensory perception recognition of the symbols on a deck of Zener cards. The test subjects attempted to identify Zener card symbols, based on card selections in a blind testing model. Research that led to an Associate Professorship and I have the right to these researched findings and he better believe it! Now is the time to confront how his outlandish research, and behaviors will surely have damaging effects toward the University. And by God, even to the field of psychology. I will not kowtow like the others in that staff meeting.

To Soule's flaunted so-called regression studies, BAH, I say! Moreover, he demeans the work of mine while suggesting that people can remember being in the womb. Really? Maybe he could go back into the womb to find out, whose research is considered the most creditable? Ha! Ha! Now Chancellor Hanson Folks is even entertaining Damon's request to develop and teach such a class. Witchcraft indeed! Somehow this outrage needs to be stopped. The authorization of such a course would place this University in jeopardy for ridicule and possible loss of accreditation.

CHAPTER SIX

Graduate School

Damon's credentials were in a different vein. He, too, had received substantial recognition, both academically and nationally. Research started in graduate school and continued to grow both in complexity and new discoveries. His primary interest was attempting to identify the development of a child's personality and influences both by his or her family genealogy influences plus external and sociological environments.

As his research developed, he began looking for external influences other than family dynamics. Thus started a quagmire attempting to decipher all the aspects of personality from birth to adulthood and beyond. During Graduate School, his initial research explicitly focused on genetic influences. Yet, he also knew this alone was less than fifty percent of the total picture.

He began explorations based on developing profiles of possible developmental stages in line with Erik and Joan Erickson's theories of psychosocial influences. He then added Piaget, Watson, and other opinions, providing him with ideas of where to look, yet none seemed to suggest a path of understanding. By the time he completed his Doctoral program, he seemed more confused than when he had started. That is when he began understanding he was walking a path of social psychology, not just pure psychology.

During the quest for a research and teaching position, he met with and participated in an interview with Dr. Hanson Folks. Up to that moment, Damon was on the verge of abandoning his passion for research. University after University all showed disdain for this passion of his. His desire for a research position was mostly ignored or just given lip service, even ridiculed. At times he was also accused of requesting an area of research that was a total waste of time and nothing but a wild goose chase.

Then he found this scholar of note, but also a possible mentor. Dr. Folks was not only interested in hiring him as an assistant professor, but also becoming an advocate for Damon's continued research. As Damon explained his desire to utilize hypnosis and meditation to explore early childhood learning, the more interest Dr. Folks exhibited. After an additional hour of exploring Damon's ideas and his research model, Dr. Folks became fully invested.

The two of them continued to discuss how regressing subjects back to their early learning experiences may increase psychological insights. One outcome might be to understand how some children were able to develop the ability to control their impulses while others were not. Both agreed that their explorations could be instrumental in discovering ways of decreasing deviant behaviors dangerous to self or others. Even more importantly to identify the source and potential and treatment of such behaviors, as antisocial and possibly even sociopathic behaviors. They hoped the research would have a high probability of identifying the dividing point between criminal behavior and socially acceptable behavior.

Initially, Damon's interest was in exploring impulse control development in two-to-five years old children. The closer he came to the elusive answers, he found himself searching farther back into childhood.

The search led to hypnotically regressing subjects, and the possibility of exploring their actual birth experiences. In time, this became the research focal point. At this hypnotic depth, some of the research subjects began reporting in-the-womb memories. Only three out of the twenty-one seemed to describe experiences suggesting possible awareness had survived through the birth experience.

Yolanda, one of the research volunteers, even reported hearing external verbalizations while still in the womb. During her debrief she explained, "I heard sounds, I think they were voices but did not understand what was being said, I just somehow understood that I was hearing voices. But Dr. D. how could I? I was a baby still in the womb?"

"My guess is from how you are describing your experience you may be remembering what is referred to as memories of the episodic type. An example would be similar to remembering visiting the beach for the first time or remembering a birthday two years ago. This was significantly different from a semantic memory of information such as a date, or someones name." He explained, then paused in time to stop himself from delving deeper into a discussion relating to his fascination with the Swiss psychotherapist Carl Jung and his theory of the collective unconscious. Jung suggested the collective unconscious was a type of genetic memory. He also believed these types of memories consisted of implicit beliefs and thoughts inherited from our ancestors. Jung's theories had not fared well when scrutinized within scientific models of research. However, it did stimulate interest in Damon's desire to develop a deeper understanding of how memories affect current behaviors.

A year later, Damon wrote a research paper related to Noam Chomsky's theories suggesting memories, at their core, had elements of genetic semantic memory. This fueled Damon's desire to focus his research on identifying how the reality of a human's sensory input is interpreted within their consciousness. Specifically how this sensory information is assembled into something we might believe is a memory. Within the psychological and sociological disciplines, controversy had been brooding for quite some time over false memories versus real memories.

Questions regarding the mysteries of the human mind were sure to have a significant impact on an extensive range of compelling topics. Such as courtroom eye-witness testimonies, in addition to therapy relating to early childhood, marital relationships, and so many other areas. The most significant issue was how to narrow the research information into a manageable scope in order to identify only the essential data.

Damon was surprised to see a significant difference between the observations described before utilizing hypnosis and those after. In some cases, differences were like the individuals were describing different occurrences.

His original research had continued to provide information, which brought up more questions. These questions increased his interest. The results of his research began gaining attention from other professors and other professionals. Thirty-two percent of his volunteer research subjects, with a high susceptibility to hypnosis, reported some possibility of past-birth memories. A tiny sample expressed some of these memories could have taken place in the womb. During debriefing these subjects explained they believed this because, "They were in the womb and that is how they knew."

When Damon combined susceptibility and meditation training, percentages climbed to thirty-six percent reported some possible past birth memories. Two percent of these subjects reported possible in-womb memories. One of the subjects also reported experiencing what they believed were past life experiences. At first, Damon ignored the small percentage of student subjects reporting in-womb and past life experiences. He even decided, for a short time, that these volunteer subjects were too unstable to be included in the research.

Rigid adherence to scientific research methods gave his research respectability. It also resulted in the encouragement to report these so-called experiences. Each step of the research seemed to uncover additional information. The study had taken on a life of its own. It was as if Damon was just along for the ride.

In some cases hypnotically induced meditative states brought startling clarity of the subject's memories of birth and life in the womb. If validated, this information had the potential to expand beliefs about the human developmental process. There seemed little doubt some of the discoveries would cause quite a stir, which genuinely excited him. What was not as exciting was concern about what the university's reaction to a new field of exploration. One that was in reality, in opposition to scientific and long accepted human capability.

Contrary to common perceptions, the academic community is not the open minded liberal thinkers they claim to be. To most people, college professors are responsible for the liberalism seen in college students. In reality, it is the students that keep professors liberal. Most universities do not cherish controversy.

The strong support of Professor Folks had reassured Damon from the very beginning of their association. His encouragement helped motivate Damon to follow wherever the experiments led. On numerous occasions, Damon found himself losing faith and allowing fear to impede the research progress. Each time it was Professor Hanson Folks pulling him back from an abyss that was only in Damon's mind. Dr. Folks was the helping hand that led him on a path of discovery instead of defeat. He cautioned Damon there were people that would believe his research was the work of the devil.

CHAPTER SEVEN

Who is Dr. Hanson Folks?

Damon had first met Dr. Hanson Folks when applying for a Magnolia University pre-doctoral research scholarship program. Almost eight years later, the two were more than student and teacher. In those years, Dr. Folks had become his teacher, research supervisor, mentor, and so much more. He was instrumental in Damon's first appointment to Associate Professor, then Assistant Professor, Full Professor, and, a true friend. Damon believed he knew Hanson Folks at a deeper level than anyone outside of his close family members.

At age twenty-two Hanson Folks first walked into the office of Chancellor Westly Grayson III to face a grueling interview conducted by Chancellor Westly and two other professors. Hanson had since seen this meeting as the real beginning of discovering his true mission in life. The experience emphasized a path against, as he put it, God, father, family, and all that was considered holy.

Folk's father had decided from the beginning of his son's young life that Hanson's destiny was to be an integral member of the family shipping business, including its web of surrounding investments. Hanson, on the other hand, decided to apply for a graduate program in Psychology. His father was initially willing to accept Hanson's choice of a major. In fact, during Hanson's undergraduate studies, father Folks believed his son's investment in psychology would lead his son to a deeper understanding of human nature. In his father's mind, this included the ability to use the increased knowledge of psychology as a tool for manipulation, benefiting the Folks Shipping Empire.

Hanson knew this was his father's assumption and felt a pang of underlying guilt as he knowingly manipulated his father. He attempted to justify his behavior yet was unable too. Even by using his psychology knowledge to ignore the guilt he felt in disappointing his father, it just did not work. As the days piled up, he genuinely began giving in to his father's desire instead of following his dream.

The Graduate School evaluations scheduled for the following day increased his guilt both for giving in to his father and, giving up his dreams. The evaluations were to be performed by the Chancellor of Marigold University School of Social Sciences. This man was known as the one most responsible for the Marigold University Psychology Department's respect and prestige. He was also the founder of the department and Hanson had to stand before him.

During the three days before meeting Chancellor Doctor Grayson, Hanson began backpedaling on his decision to participate in the prospective evaluation. Each of his internal discussions started by invalidating his ability. Plus, his lack of respect for his father's wishes. However, mostly he began to doubt his own very capable intellect and wondered if he had the strength to achieve such a lofty goal. This internal discussion continued to rotate between, "Yes, I Can! What right does Damon have? True, true, Damon has to go along with father's wants. What do they want?"

His negative self-talk continued right up to, the moment of dread as he entered the doors of the Chancellor's office. Practicing deep breathing exercises, he approached the den of terror. He stammered his name to the receptionist who appeared to have a true smile, as she replied,

"Why yes, we have been expecting you, but not for, well, let us see," as she looked up at the clock on the wall, "Not for another 48 minutes or so."

He just stared, his mind blank, mouth partway open as if beginning to respond, when the still smiling receptionist asked, "Would you like to come back in about thirty minutes or so? The alternative is that the gentleman may have a seat and wait."

Hanson could not remember his response or how he managed three flights of stairs leading to the outside. His mind seemed to wait in the background until his mouth exclaimed, "Shit!" Loudly as several students paused to look at him while others sitting on benches or the grass turned their heads. As his mouth began to voice another profanity, his mind took hold and he stooped in time.

Thirty-two minutes later, he was waiting on the bench outside of the Chancellor's office. The nice receptionist a short time later announced, "The Chancellor will see the gentleman" and ushered him into the conference room.

A gray-haired man with large horn-rim glasses sat at the head of the table. He seemed to be nearly swallowed up behind the massive mahogany conference table. He introduced himself as Chancellor Grayson and introduced the two additional men sitting on each side of him. His voice was powerful and deep-toned. So much so, it startled Hanson as if it was coming from somewhere other than the diminutive man.

That same voice directed Candidate Hanson Folks to take a seat at the opposite end of the table, and the interrogation began:

"Professor Grant, you may question the candidate."

The robust gentleman on Dr. Grayson's right softly cleared his throat. Then he asked Candidate Folks to explain in detail what he could contribute to the field of Psychology. Next, the slim younger man on the left asked Hanson to explain…

Chancellor Grayson observed the questions and answers and their nervous Candidate with a mild air of indifference. That is, for the first hour and fifteen minutes. Then with what appeared to be a stern look, he stood up, strode around the table, began to smile and held out his hand, saying, "Well, young man as your advisor, I strongly suggest you meet me Monday at 10 AM," as he was shaking Hanson's sweaty hand.

Three years and eight months later, The Magnolia Psychology Department was receiving even more acclaim. In part spotlighted by Chancellor Grayson's brilliant Ph.D. research candidate Hanson Folks. A student who not only earned the newly recognized Doctorate of Philosophy with an emphasis in Psychology and also as a result of his research had instituted a change in the research field of personality development.

It was Chancellor Grayson's suggestion that Dr. Folks began exploring the realm of human susceptibility from childhood to adulthood. The Chancellor was a very persuasive man, and unlike most of his colleges, he was not afraid of controversy. His encouragement pushed Hanson Folks to explore uncharted areas of psychology. This challenged Folk's determination and inspired his intuitive intellect in new and fertile directions of research. It also highlighted his unique ability of seeing what many others could not see.

Initially he was confused with Chancellor Grayson's questioning in relation to susceptibility and its ability to effect personality development. Pausing for a few moments while analyzing how being susceptible to diseases could be related to personality, he then confronted his mentor.

"Chancellor, I am at somewhat of a loss. I know serious childhood diseases affect a child's personality, but we are talking about a relatively small sampling. I am invested in understanding personality development in, well, from a range of aspects… primarily what are the effects of birth order, gender, mother, father, cultural heritage, and so on?"

"I believe you are circling the issues, Dr. Hanson. Let me rephrase the ingredients? Why are children from the same parents similar yet so very different? How do they develop significantly different personalities? How does this happen?"

"Well, they have different experiences, and one child may be more influenced by one parent while child two may be more identified with the other or perhaps someone not in the immediate family…wait, you are questioning what it is that creates… Let me rephrase a girl child may be more susceptible to learning female behaviors from her mother and the son is more prone to learn male behaviors from his father. Their specific genetic characteristics make a difference also!

"You are testing my susceptibility to your input over my own, or another professor, or even Freud, Jung, or even Maslow. You are my mentor, you are a Chancellor you are… Holy Smokes I believe I understand the concept, just the same I need to explore this in much more detail. My mind is spreading out like a spider web. I mean threads of multiple directions, and connections, I am somewhat hesitant to ask yet I need to, I guess stop and think. Susceptibility… damn, well, sorry about that. I did not mean to curse."

"Your words were not offensive to me. The concept we are exploring has an incredible amount of facets. The critical one is are we susceptible to the belief systems we live with and participate in such as our social and family environment? We also need to add our emotions, disappointments and, well so many more into infinity? I not only excuse your need to terminate our discussion I encourage it too. I have one recommendation, identify your initial starting point by attempting to analyze the amount of times during this discussion you were, let me say susceptible to your beliefs vice my belief systems. On other note you also need to consider your tendency to be motivated by emotion, vice analytical based responses."

As time passed, Dr. Folk's reputation grew and he earned an Associate Professorship position. Eighteen months later, he was becoming recognized as one of the foremost experts in the relatively new field of sociological influences on personality development.

Hanson Folks also made waves in 1932, in another direction by wedding Miss Barbara Camoran of the Camoran Communications Empire. Mother and Father Camoran believed their daughter had chosen below her station. The one saving grace was how Hanson demonstrated an intensity suggesting he had every likelihood of becoming highly successful.

The first time Barbara brought him home to meet "The Parents," Hanson had just completed his second Bachelors's Degree. Father Camoran seemed impressed with a young man that showed enough discipline to earn degrees in both Biology and Psychology by the age of 24. He was even more impressed when Hanson announced his wish to continue his studies. Then he proudly proclaimed he had been accepted as a candidate for a Masters in Psychology.

All went well until it was unveiled Hanson had lost the financial support of his family. All because he was pursuing further education instead of taking his rightful place in the family's very successful Folks Shipping Company. Now it was abundantly clear he did not have a way to support their daughter, and just when the two had started talking about marriage.

When it was further discovered, Barbara was to support the two of them on her family provided yearly allowance, the strain became verbal and angry. This proved to be just the beginning of the hostility, which seemed to grow each time a new encounter or announcement was made.

Two years later, during their daughter's party celebrating Hanson's recent graduation Barbara announced, the arrogant young freeloader was now a candidate for postgraduate studies in research Psychology. Both behaved as if completing his MS in psychology with an emphasis on the sociological impacts on human behavior justified his continued disregard for a need to earn a living.

With immense pride, Barbara stood proudly proclaiming to all the assembled guests that her fiancé graduated at the top of his class. This was greeted with a loud round of applause and renewed congratulations. Mother Camoran had to choke back a retort, it was just too much. She was now convinced more than ever Hanson was using them as a free ticket.

He was just a professional student and would end up spending most of his life in school. Heaven's sakes, it was time for him to start providing for her daughter. If not in the shipping business, then he needed to start learning the Camoran Communications business. It was damn well time he became responsible for supporting their daughter. He could only accomplish this if only he quit this foolishness and got on with his life. He darn well needs to stop all this fiddle/faddle school stuff.

The Camerons family, their daughter, and especially Hanson, became estranged without openly acknowledging such. Hans used his research and studies as a way to avoid interactions, and the Camerons mainly refrained from being available. They tended to be out of town on business, vacations, or visiting other family members and or friends. When occasions made it unavoidable to stay clear they managed to avoid each other, and all parties behaved in an outwardly civil manner.

CHAPTER EIGHT

The Journey Begins

Unlike his father and the Camerons, Professor Grayson was actively committed to his Doctoral candidate and pushed and prodded Hanson toward literature reviews in the field of personality development. For Hanson, this seemed a nudge towards moving backward instead of new areas of knowledge. After numerous and sometimes heated discussions between Professor Grayson and himself, Hanson began to formulate intersections between existing research and new avenues that were coalescing into new insights.

The majority of assessments he had studied and a few he had attempted to develop were based on self-reports of the research by the subjects. Their experiences naturally covered a wide range of previous unknown variables, with the people participating as research subjects and those conducting the research. Some of the researchers were attempting to define the nature of personality. Others were trying to understand the deep secrets of how personality developed. He acknowledged to himself the many years he had been traveling this same path.

His research design needed to look at both the objective and subjective criteria if he wanted to study personality. By placing objective criteria in the model, it would lead to the beginning of identifying significant breakthroughs in assessing and understanding human nature. If he could only identify a spectrum of measurable traits via objective criteria, it would be possible to cross-reference these across a wide range of subjective criteria.

Thus he believed it would revolutionize the field of personality assessment.

More importantly, this method could make new inroads in understanding the what, how, and why of personality. Thus began Hanson Folks Doctoral Dissertation. Advancing a new point of view based on this research would validate his Thesis. He was nearing completion of the third year of doctoral studies. The data was in and it identified a significant paradigm shift necessary for understanding personality.

Looking down at his quivering hands, still perched above his typewriter. He was unsure if they were quivering because of the ten hours of nearly non-stop typing or because he had finished. It might need some cleaning up, but damn, his Thesis was validated, the dissertation proved it. A road had opened that would change his life from a confused student trying to find directions to follow, to being a scientist with a specific purpose.

Pounding on the apartment door broke into his reverie just as his wife shouted,

"What's happening? Is someone hurt? WHAT?"

Hanson jumped to his feet and looked around. She was staring at him, then the door, then just staring at him as he grabbed her in a bear hug shouting

"I did it! I did It!" carrying her with him as he asked the door,

"Who is it?" and heard the neighbor's voice say, "Are you all right?"

Two days later, his Thesis Supervisor accepted his Thesis manuscript for review. Five days followed full of anxiety and self-doubt. Hanson was sweating, praying, and filling the hours until Professor Grayson finally summoned him. As soon as he sat down, the Professor began reviewing areas needing clarification. For what seemed like hours the interrogation continued. Hanson's stomach started aching and he could feel sweat trickling down from his armpits as he addressed each area the Professor was addressing. Without a doubt sure his dissertation was in the process of being rejected.

The Professor paused for what seemed an eternity while Hanson waited for the rejection. Finally, the Professor stood up, so he did also. Hanson began to formulate a plea to redo his research. Then as his mouth opened, the Professor stated,

"Your dissertation will now be submitted for the *viva voce* examination. It will be an honor to represent Doctor Hanson and his research conclusions. I must say this Professor is proud of the work, dedication, and, most of all, the conclusions my protégé has arrived at." All Hanson managed was a stammering, "Thank you, Professor."

Three days later, he responded to a summons to Doctor Westly Grayson III office. After Hanson was seated DoctorGrayson stated,

"After I reviewed your experimental methodology, and the conclusions derived, my first response was, this Candidate's work is exceptional. Now I am very pleased to say it will be my honor to award and address you as Doctor Folks."

Dr. Grayson then stood and walked around his desk holding out a hand and taking Hans hand in a firm grip and said,

"Damn if this is not the epitome of what the term Doctoral Thesis stands for! Doctor Hanson, without question, you have something here, son!"

Hanson felt a shiver of goosebumps creep up his arms and on to his cheeks. His dreams were coming true. His mind kept flying around like a whirlwind while trying to focus on Dr. Grayson being impressed.

Later after leaving Dr. Grayson office, Hanson out loud stated proudly to the world,

"I, Doctor Hanson Folks is Good! I mean, exceptionally good, Barbara will be proud of me, thinking (Oh shit what about her

Mother?) Nevertheless, one thing is for sure I am no longer a Doctoral Candidate. This man is now Doctor Folks,"

All this was twisting and twisting, around and around in his mind. Until he just started running, running to meet Barbara and tell her the news. His mind continued spinning until he found her, their arms flew around each other, and he began to sob with joy, relief and most of all excitement.

"What the hell are you blubbering about," Barbara demanded with excitement, less than his but still being infected with his joy and knowing it was something about Hans and his Doctoral studies and was there something about money, and… her Mother???

They talked for what seemed a long time, mainly Hanson explaining their good fortune. Something that Barbara was unsure would be her good fortune, considering it was pretty clear she would be the one dealing with her Mother. A mother that wanted Hanson to start a career and start being paid. Besides, starting to become a member of the family and yes, also the family business. However, clearly what was happening indicated that Hanson was being encouraged to develop this experimental model and prep it for a presentational concept for the Department of War.

That's when she abruptly broke into his reverie,

"Do you have any idea how my Mother will react to the news that not only are you wanting to continue your research at the university? But you also want to talk to the War Department?"

"I have been trying to tell you I will no longer be a student. I am a Doctor and will have an Adjunct Professor position. That is until your husband Doctor Hanson Folks is approved for a position as an Assistant professor."

"But what about Mother, After all this and so much money?"

Hanson just looked at her in shock, stuttered,

"I, ah, I hope to get a grant from the DOW, you know the Department of War…I, ah, ah, It will work out…" then he turned and walked away slumped shouldered. She just didn't hear. As he put on his coat and moved to the door, a scream of excitement ripped the silence, and he spun to…

"You what?" she shouted, "you are what, and going to do what, and, and…"

52

CHAPTER NINE

History of PaPa

During the long drive to Aisling House, Damon began rehearsing what to say to Hanson. Really how much not to say. The Aisling was not just a dwelling for a very wealthy man and his family. It was more. Maybe it was more akin to a love story in a novel or movie. As it had a long and intriguing history that began when his father, Fredrick, met his Love. It started when Frederick was of a similar age as Yolanda and Dean. His history with any luck would draw Fredrick into the original story of Yolanda and the second part of how Dean fits into the picture.

Fredrick's childhood had been divided between visiting cities along the northern coast of California and the rest of North America, their estate Aisling House outside of San Francisco, and attending private schools. Until his tenth birthday, Fredrick was regulated to remain at Aisling or school. Even when at neither location, he spent time exploring the local areas with his mother or brothers. He seldom saw his father other than at the dinner table when he was dining with the family in-between engagements or at the "OFFICE" as Fredrick liked to refer to it.

At a very early age, Fredrick was fascinated by all the different peoples and their histories. The Spanish, Italian fisherman, and Chinese were the most intriguing as their way of speaking and dressing was quite unique. He often fantasized about becoming an explorer and, by the age of eleven, spent almost as much time sitting and observing the people, countrysides, and towns as all other activities combined. San Francisco in the late 1800's and early 1900's was at the top of the list for exploring.

His fascination was a constant annoyance to his father Quinn, who had dreamed of a son that would be fascinated by ships and the shipping business. He loved his son very much, yet his love of the sea and ships never seemed to rub off on his son. He tried stimulating interest in the Folks shipping empire by taking Fredrick on a Folks merchant ship. Then on the family yacht Nollaig, named after his mother. Instead his son was always paying more attention to people, places, and things.

Quinn's wife Saoirse suggested his father, Sinead, would be more than willing to educate young Frederick in the family history of ships and the seas. Both Grandfather and Grandson thought this was a great idea. Fredrick would always be spit and polished 20 or 30 minutes before he was ready for PaPa to sit down with him. He was a grand storyteller. Even when Fredrick had heard some of his stories three, four, or even more times. Thus every Thursday right after PaPa's lunch nap, he would call for young Fredrick, which he had nicknamed Drick.

Quinn had vigorously attempted to teach Fredrick to always address his Father, as Grandfather or Sir one or the other. His Grandfather, Grandmother, and Mother openly opposed this scenario by stating firmly they preferred PaPa instead of Grandfather and Grams instead of Grandmother. Father's really galling moment came when PaPa sitting at the dinner table said,

"And by the way, my nickname for the boy is not Rick. It is, in fact, Drick, did we not agree that was a great nickname," smiling over the table at Fredrick. A small choking sound came from Quinn, and a quiet giggle slipped out from Saoirse. Quinn had clearly lost that battle, yet was determined to win his son's interest in ships and the shipping business.

Quinn's father, Sinead, was the first in the family tradition of ship captains and ship owners. He had begun as a cabin boy at age 12 on a local merchant ship that transported cargo up and down the coast of Ireland from Cork to Dublin. Shortly after his fourteenth birthday, he signed on with a packet ship as a deckhand. This continued over many voyages, and by the age of twenty, he had worked his way up to the third mate. Unlike most of his shipmates, he was extremely frugal with his wages and dreamed of having his own ship. PaPa's history clearly elevated his young grandson's interest in the sea.

So it was that every Thursday afternoon, the two would meet in the resident library. Sitting in the overstuffed leather chairs, young Drick curled up in one and PaPa sat close to the fireplace with a pipe in hand. With the fire crackling, PaPa with his brandy, Drick sitting with a cup of steaming tea and bright eyes waiting for the sea's story to begin.

It began with PaPa describing a picture of the Ireland he grew up in some seventy years past.

"We ere poor folk, living in a poor land that grew potatoes, ate potatoes, and hoped to sell potatoes. Each day was a hungry day as we had little else, the funny thing was we didn't know we were hungry as much as just tired. The first time I rode in the back of a wagon with my Pa and our two sacks of potatoes was my first great adventure. I hardly knew over two hours had passed, because of all I saw.

So many people that looked much like us, yet as we continued it changed to people dressed better walking and riding magnificent horses or riding in wagons of their own. Passing people that were begging, hands outstretched, or just sitting in the dust as we passed by. Most everybody paid little or even no notice like they were not seeing these poor souls. I asked my Dadai about them, and he told me they were those without land. No land, no potatoes.

Then I saw tall tree trunks out in the distance and asked Dadai what happened to their leaves. He told me they were the masts on ships. I remember being confused, I knew very little about ships and could not understand why they had funny looking trees that Dadai said were not trees. I knew I had to see what these mysterious things were, that lived on what he said was the sea.

We continued along the dusty path into more and more people. Crowded buildings side by side. The noise grew as we continued toward town the din grew louder each minute. Horses, mules, carts, wagons, and people yelling. At first, I wanted to duck down close my eyes, and cover my ears, …but at the same time, I could not stop looking. I was being transported to a new land, a place I had never imagined.

Shortly after this, we sold our potatoes, and not long after, I saw a sight that overtook me. Something I have never forgotten, something that changed my life. There were ships and water as far as you could see. Ships in the distance with cloud-like things attached to the trees without leaves. To this day, I don't recall what Dadai and I did until we were leaving for the journey back home. I know that I could not stop pestering him for answers about everything. A lot of that Dadai did not know, which I did not think, he did not know.

One thing I did know, I was coming back to this place. I would learn about people I did not know existed, places I knew nothing about, and ships that could take me to places I wanted to know. I had a purpose, and it was to travel the sea. Dadai, Mathair, and my two dearthairs tired of my endless questions and thoughts about the sea. Dadai stopped taking me to this place and took one or both of my dearthairs instead. Instead of this decreasing my dreams, instead it made them stronger.

For the next two years, I dreamed and planned. Every time anyone would listen, I would beg for more information. I did not care much about what information. I just wanted to know anything about people, places, and how to find out more. Against my Mathair's protests, Dadai arranged a surprise for my 12th birth year. He took me to town, to the ships at the docks and a man named Conor McCarthy.

After Dadai greeted him, he introduced me, took my shoulders in his, locked eyes with me, and asked, "Do you still dream about being on a ship? Make sure you are sure in your answer as this will be your one and only chance."

I stammered and stuttered. Unsure of what was happening while my heart was pumping so hard, I was not sure I could answer. Then I spoke the words that changed my world, yes, Dadai, more than anything in life. He had a bedroll in the back of the wagon he asked me to fetch, shook my hand, turned his back, and walked away.

"Well, boy," Mister McCarthy called, get your ass up the plank, and for the first time, I stepped aboard a ship. I was a cabin boy, whatever that meant, but I knew I wanted to see the world.

When PaPa finished this first part, Fredrick began wondering if mother manipulated father into allowing Grandfather to help Fredrick follow his dreams. She must have known how Grandfather dreamed of things that his father had not. How much it must have hurt Grandfather's Father's heart watching his son turn away from the family and embrace the life of a seaman. An experience that brought him to the Americas, so far removed from Ireland.

Grandfather had shared how painful it was when his own father stayed in Ireland during the days of starvation. The potatoes were diseased, people were rioting, and fighting to get on any ship, taking them to a better place. Grandfather, by this time, was part owner and the Master of the Packet Ship *Breeze Farraige*.

He returned home to Cork and pleaded with his father to gather the family and board his ship for America. His father refused, saying,

"Ireland is my home, and I will not desert her. Like you! And now you are asking me to be like you. You are no son of mine." His mother was standing back in the kitchen area with tears running down her cheeks, looking away as his father demanded that he leave.

In the following years, Grandfather Sinead made five voyages to Ireland to bring people to New York. In the beginning, he was making a significant profit. The cargo loaded for England and other ports were mainly cotton, tobacco, furs, skins, salt meat, flaxseed, rice, tar, turpentine, and pitch. Also, a surprisingly high number of passengers were willing to book passage on these same voyages leaving for those ports.

The cargo when we were retuning to Ireland filled all the cargo spaces in addition to high paying passengers in first class and immigrants in steerage. Grandfather made a significant profit from the cargo going both directions along with a good profit from the passengers booked going east to European ports and broke even with passengers traveling to North American ports.

Anger toward Irish immigrants began to boil over by the 1850s. It also began affecting his ability to procure enough cargo to continue making enough profit. He decided to sail the Atlantic coast in search of less hostile environments for freight. Florida's principal ports became the primary area that he worked. Shipping vast quantities of cargo such as citrus fruits, cotton, and lumber all along the Atlantic coast and as far south as the Caribbean islands. For years the profits soared, and he began to believe it was time to purchase *Breeze Farraige* outright from the other owners.

Returning from New Orleans with cargo holds filled to the brim plus thirty-six well-paying passengers, he brought the *Breeze Farraige* past Tybee Island, looking forward to some shore time. It would take a month or more in Savanna for needed repairs. If he was honest, his body could use some too, starting with a long soapy bath. He, along with First Mate Johansen, would switch off with the second mate for shore leave.

The day after mooring, Grandfather Sinead made ready to depart the *Breeze*, stopped, and insured a work crew would be checking in with his First Mate ready to begin work. He then left the ship and strode toward the Pirates Inn and Tavern for a tankard of ale or a shot or two of whiskey, a good, meal, hot bath, and a soft bed.

The next day he walked the waterfront and watched the seagulls before heading back to the Pirates Inn. When he discovered a place to perch on and observe the *Breeze Farraige*, off in the distance. It was a pleasant spot to make himself comfortable with an excellent view of the waterfront and the shops lining it.

The sun was warming, the gulls singing their song, and a light breeze lulling him sleepy. Sometime later, he knew not how long, a kink had woke him. Pushed himself up from the log he was resting against and started working the kinks out. Stretching and yawning, he looked around and glanced toward his ship then down the waterfront. Not far in the distance, a woman caught his attention. Standing on a long spit of sand, she was just looking out to the harbor, just standing as if transfixed by the view. Maybe ten or twelve minutes passed, and still she did not move. Finally, she turned and walked back to the path leading away.

After another good night's sleep, plenty of food, and a need to move around, he walked in the direction of yesterday's log. Unaware he was doing it, he looked toward where she had been the day before. No one was there. Well, that was uncomfortable, he thought, becoming aware of a pang of disappointment. Found the log, began to move around it to find a place to sit, looked up before sitting down, and observed a female walking.

She was moving in a direction that might lead to the sand spit. Unsure if this was the same person, he continued in his movement to sit, but at the same time to watch. She was too far away to tell age, or much else. Her headscarf covered a lot of her long dark, maybe black hair that fell free from the bottom, and a breeze waved it gently. She turned in the direction of the spit and soon was in the same area as yesterday. Again just staring over at the water in what seemed a longing.

That caused a flush of embarrassment, he was sure would redden his cheeks. He made himself look away as if to prove he was not staring. It did not last long before he was again staring at her staring. Never did she look his way. This continued until like the day before she turned and walked the same direction as the last time. He guessed it was about twenty minutes since he heard four bells ringing on ships in the harbor, so it was 2 o'clock. Then he heard the sound of three bells ring out, so it had been at the most maybe ten minutes before 2:30.

Right at two bells the next day, he was in his seat watching. Not long after, he saw a figure way off in the distance walking towards the spot. A slight flush of excitement crept over him as the figure became female and turned toward her spot. She once again began standing and staring.

Sinead knew he would return tomorrow, for what he was not sure, but he would. He arrived at precisely two bells and, instead of stopping, kept walking. While attempting not to appear interested in her, her beauty took him by surprise. She was not looking at him but seemed to be avoiding eye contact altogether, as if afraid. He was not paying attention to where he was walking and stumbled with a slight yelp, trying not to fall. She just kept walking. Too embarrassed to do anything else, he kept walking.

Not knowing where he was going but a short while later discovered a local market place, browsed around, and then bought an apple. He found a bench, sat down, took a bite, and tried to come up with a way to introduce himself when and if he saw her again.

Knowing he would, he got to his feet, bought another apple, and began to retrace his steps back.

He saw her in the distance coming his way, stepped off the path, and walked between two tattered and weathered shacks. He went around behind and back to the other side, to see if she walked past. He spent the next few minutes, chiding himself for behaving like he didn't know what, maybe just a dumb Irish bumbler. He looked back around the edge of the shack and saw her walking toward the market.

Hoping no one would see him hiding, he watched as she gathered many things, using her headscarf as a pouch to carry everything, she hurried away from the market down the path. He wanted to follow, but it seemed too obvious and he did not want her to think he was up to no good. He decided to drag his stinking ass back to the inn. Maybe to have something to eat, have enough ale to forget how backwoods he was behaving, and go to bed.

The next day at two bells he was once again waiting to… something…but what. Right on time, she was walking toward him. Oh, blarney, she was walking past the spot. Right towards him. Right up in front of him. Sparkling big green eyes looking directly into his and said, "Sir is there a reason you keep watching me?"

He stammered, stuttered, coughed, and then answered,

"I, I saw you looking at the sea, and," he realized he was speaking in Gaelic, shut his mouth, as she responded in Gaelic,

"And that gives you permission to stare, follow, and what else?" The look on his face must have touched a humor spot that resulted in her laughing from the heart. A smile seemed to take over her entire face, and they both began to laugh.

She invited him to follow, and they both walked out on the sandpit, looked to the sea, and began to talk. He introduced himself and told her he was from Cork, and his ship was the *Breeze Farraige*. Tears fell from her eyes as she said,

"My name is Nollaig and this is where I come to taste the salt in the air and pretend I am free to leave this place."

Then said she had to go, as she began turning to leave. She stopped, looked back at him, not wiping the tears and quietly said,

"And..."

Without knowing what to say, his tongue and lips said,

"I will be here."

Each day he was there, she was not, and then on the fourth day she was waiting before he was there.

"It is too painful, and too hard. You come and go as you please. All I can do is look at the sea and yearn to go. This is where I yearn so no one can see. Now you are here, and my heart grieves." All he could do was take her in his arms and hold her as she grieved. In bits and pieces, her story began to unfold. She could only be with him for 15-20 minutes, which is how she started.

"My mother died giving me birth. My Dadai was killed because he was Irish and blamed for bringing yellow fever. When I was four years of age, and my brother was ten, we escaped to Tybee Island, and the *Euchee* Indians took us in. We lived with them until an alligator killed my brother. An Indian named Mother Soswa took me to Savanna and left me on the steps of a church." She paused for a long moment, looking toward the sea and said,

"I have to leave. If I'm ever late, I won't be allowed to get fruits and vegetables from the market." Her green eyes began to tear, and she turned and began to almost run. Sinead could only stand and watch, feeling helpless, which was not something he had ever learned to be.

Each day they spent their 15-20 minutes on the spit as her story continued to unfold. At an intense level, she was treated the same as the household slaves. She was indentured to the Gustean family for taking her in, even if it was to be treated as a slave.

Back aboard the *Breeze*, Sinead began ensuring and inspecting the ship's repairs, preparing the vessel to sail around South America to San Fransisco, California. The *Breeze* was ready now to start loading cargo and supplies needed to survive such a dangerous voyage.

Now he had to concentrate on the task at hand. Instead, his thoughts were, how in hades can he tell Nollaig he was leaving. He would have to tell her soon, but how?

He put it off for two additional days and knew he was running out of time. The loading was in progress, the Breeze was seaworthy, and it would be at the most three more weeks before getting under way. With a heart of sorrow, he walked down the gangplank and began pushing himself toward the spit. It was time to break her heart. She, who was yearning to go. He who had to go and both of them were helpless.

He was waiting when she arrived. She immediately understood something was terribly wrong, but could not ask. As he told her, she seemed to shrink into herself. The sparkling eyes begin dimming, and she was unable to look at him. When he was finished, she was sobbing and shaking. Once again, he took her in his arms as she clung to him and sagged in his arms. Tears flowed from them both as they held on to each other.

Through the sobs, she began to whisper something he could not hear. Her body straightened, as she put a hand on each side of his face, and looked into his eyes,

"Please take me with you." she said.

He quit breathing, trying to let his mind catch what his ears were hearing. The two connected, and he was the one almost sagging to the ground. A minute passed, or it could be an hour, it did not matter.

"How?" was all he could say.

"I can meet you here and get on the Breeze, and, and well, go with you."

"We have to talk, I don't know, I have passengers, What will the Gustean's do, do they know. Do any of my passengers know you? What would they do if they caught you? I could not bear bringing danger to you."

"Are you afraid. Do you not want it? I mean, I thought you, ah, oh God, please help me."

She started to cry, turned from him, and began to run. It was a second before he knew he could not, would not leave her. "Stop, please, stop, he began yelling and running as fast as he could. With a last spurt of speed he caught her arm and spun her around. They collided, stumbling, and fell to the ground. He landing almost on top of her, barely breaking his fall with his hand and knees.

"If you don't want me, I will not beg; Please let me go, please," and then his lips met hers.

Until the day he was to set sail, they met, planned, and held each other during their precious fifteen minutes.

The day was overcast and windy, an easterly. It would assist them out of the harbor and into the open ocean. One of the last passengers to come aboard was a slim black-haired lad with green eyes. He was greeted by the ship's Master and escorted to a cabin. He was a person seldom seen and ate alone in his cabin. It was said he suffered from seasickness. The passengers quickly forgot the lad as they attempted to adjust to their own bouts of seasickness, the close quarters, constant clatter of seamen going about their business.

As the voyage continued, the crew became aware that the ship's Master had his own cabin boy. Rumors flew and eventually there began to be whispering by the passengers about his cabin boy. Because of the dangerousness of rounding South America's tip no one was going to question the Captain's choice of companion.

Months later, a weathered, battered and tattered *Breeze Farraige* limped into San Francisco Bay. Abandoned ships were scattered throughout the bay. Sinead dropped anchor around a mile out from what he reckoned was the town of San Francisco. He had the mate drop the whaler to explore what may have happened. The *Breeze* had received word of the Gold Rush of 1848. It had not heard of an epidemic that could be responsible for all of the deserted ships. They hailed a group of men as they neared the wharf. As they approached even closer, one of the men yelled through a bull-horn to back off. It was clear something was terribly wrong.

What was wrong was gold fever. Passengers and crews were deserting their ships to search for gold. San Francisco did not want any more invading the town and causing trouble. Despite everything, the Breeze needed berthing. There were arguments everywhere they attempted to land. Finally, they beached the whaler, and Sinead began walking and questioning strangers until he gathered enough directions to continue sailing up the harbor to the north. A settlement named Vallejo seemed the most desirable.

Then came the day PaPa was not waiting in the library. Grams was sitting in PaPa's chair and asked Drick to sit down beside her. His stomach began to hurt, and Gram's eyes made the hurt worse.

"PaPa won't be coming in here anymore my heart, PaPa can't walk this far, he hurts too much. He would be delighted if you would visit him in his bed-chamber." The boy Drick, fighting to hold back his tears, stood up and thought about PaPa walking up the gangway to a world he did not know. Now he, Drick, was walking down a hallway to face something he did not want to know. Entering the room, he tried with all the strength his young heart had, to pretend everything was all right, so did PaPa. The story continued with Drick sitting beside the bed.

When Grandfather was too weak to speak, Drick would read stories to him. Drick's favorite was *Moby Dick* by Herman Melville, and surprisingly Grandfather's was *The Adventures of Huckleberry Finn* by Mark Twain. This was the last of Grandfather's storytelling of how he met Mhamo Grandmother Nollaig. One of Fredrick's longest-held wishes was that Grandfather lived long enough to tell the complete story. The story of how the home they built so long ago and named Aisling House had come to be.

Instead, Grandfather's last words a week before he passed away were,

"I pray," long pause,

"You find," a break so long Fredrick began to rise from his chair to summons help when he heard a long sigh, cough and said the last words Drick would hear from his precious Grandfather, "Promise you will find your true love."

PART TWO

CHAPTER ONE

Who Am I?

"Yolanda/YoYo/DAR who am I, what am I, am I insane? Who in the hell is DAR? Maybe I need some kind of treatment!" The more she ruminated on this and so many other unanswered questions, the more she knew something had to change. Dean was gone, school is gone, I'm lost. Crazy dreams, thoughts, visions, what the hell is happening. Can't ask Dr. D. he would think I was insane, maybe I am. All this and more began flooding through her mind after the day of the fight, how could he leave, and then join the Navy? So he could?? Do all the terrible things I have been fighting against, WHY?

Escape to think, escape to where... spun through Yolanda's mind. Run was all she could think to do. "I have to go, go where. Just go," flew through her thoughts as she piled clothes in a bag. Then she grabbed her keys. Once in the car, she just drove, not knowing where or why she just drove. Hours later, or maybe it was just minutes, a uniformed man was asking,

"What is your reason for visiting Mexico?"

The shock of crossing the border seemed to make some sense. She could only think and be, here in a place where no one was pulling on her, no one was trying to fix her, she could just be with her.

She drove until she was having trouble staying awake; and found a hotel room in Rosario a small town on the West Coast of Baja, Mexico. When she awoke confused and unsure of the day and location, she opened the shutter and discovered an incredible ocean view. For several days she only left the room to eat, other than that she slept, paced, and stared out the window at the ocean. Rosario, she discovered, was a short distance south of Tijuana, which must have been where she crossed the border.

Yolanda had no concept of how long she had driven, where she may have stayed, or what she had done after leaving the apartment. What she did remember was confusion. Fear and an overpowering desire to run from an Owl, Dr. D., or was it Dean, and whatever pulled her further into a void she did not understand.

She was flying, an Owl was guiding, and a strange woman was teaching her. Teaching about her core, the core of her being, about who and what she is, has been, will be???. Yolanda woke up from? Was it a dream, a hallucination, a vision, what the FUCK was it! She was not sure if she had screamed in her head, outside of her head, both or neither of them?

Someone, no, the teacher, the See-er, showed her, a blanket that was? Was it the way? Yolanda was not Yolanda. She was Dances-as-Rain? No, that wasn't right; it was her core, her sexuality, her being, she was woman, not man.

She was going to be a Walker? A *Thread Walker*. She had to embrace the core of her sexuality. Yolanda left her room, stalking. She was a warrior, and she would conquer. In what seemed like a daze, she began the hunt. The trance wasn't a daze; it was a razor-sharp focus, a hunter's focus. She had to hunt but did not know what. She was just pursuing.

As she hunted, she knew it was what she had to do. She had to find Who? What? Why? As of yet, she did not know. Then there was a target. A man, a macho Latino man, somehow she knew he too was on the prowl. He was looking for prey. She knew now what her prey was to be. Leaving the beach, she returned to the room. Without knowing she began to move into a trance state, her inside sight narrowed into a beam surrounding the man, the man that would be waiting on the sand at the beach. He is waiting for her when she arrives.

The moon glittered across the water, highlighting the crashing waves as they rolled gently and caressingly over the footsteps leading into the dusk. Soft moans float across the rippling sand like a lover's breath. The moans begin building in intensity until an animal-like growl erupts from Yolanda's/Dances-as-Rain's throat. The explosive climax forcing her breaths to come in rasping gasps. Looking down on the handsome man, a look of pure triumph flashed across her beautiful face. Then standing up, she stared at the moon. A smile flickered at the corners of her full lips. The young man gazed up at her. Drops of his offerings fell from between her legs and landed on his chest. Without looking down, she bent over and lifted her bikini off the golden sand, stepped over him, and like a jungle tigress, disappeared into the distance as if hunting new prey.

Yolanda had left the hotel. Then she returned to her room, not the someone who had left. This woman changed her clothes found her car, then left behind the woman who had brought the car to this place. She drove away not just a woman but as a person of power.

The university, Maggie U was unimportant, what was important, was making a difference. It was time to change from a participant in the demonstrations to the organizer. To stand in front, not be lost in the crowd. Civil rights were incredibly overdue. Color did not matter, only the person mattered. A person's religion or where they were born does not matter. Only the person matters.

CHAPTER TWO

What The Hell Was Happening?

So much had changed since then, beliefs and behaviors. This war had split the nation into the anti-war doves versus the pro-war hawks, the world view, and the loss of Dean's participation in the regression studies. Damon's incredible advances in research of early childhood memories were directly related to the involvement of Yolanda and Dean. It had developed over more than two years. The two became instrumental in what had all the earmarks of pre-birth memory formation.

Dean was far from an ideal subject, yet he and Yolanda became the catalyst and primary research subjects. Without a doubt, she was the quintessential student volunteer subject for a hypnotic age regression study, but this only became apparent after Yolanda refused to continue without Dean sitting beside her. She demanded that he not only sit beside her, he was also to hold her hand during the entirety of the hypnotic regression. She adamantly claimed it was the only way she felt safe to journey more in-depth in her regression. Up to that date, Yolanda had only been able to regress to a four or five years old.

Dr. D had assumed the request was related to the vulnerability she felt with only him. This hypothesis was somewhat proven when Dean held her hand. For the first time, she appeared to enter into a very early stage of the birth experience. This was an incredible breakthrough, research literature before this had been sparse except for only a few anecdotal claims. Now Professor Damon Soule was stepping through the door of scientific-based research that would indicate consciousness before the actual birth experience.

Just as he began to step through that door, the floor fell out below him. During the last week of Spring Quarter, Yolanda and Dean's relationship exploded into a million pieces. Two weeks later, Yolanda knocked on his office door. Looking bedraggled and lost as she stumbled in. His first thoughts were that she had been sick, or in an accident, or maybe accosted.

She appeared unable to look him in the eye, as she began to sob, "Dean is gone, he…he left me, I, I…we fought, and he left. I haven't seen him for weeks. Then I got a letter, he wrote. He joined the Navy. I didn't know what to do. All I thought was to RUN! And run, I just got back from Mexico. And I still don't know what to do,"

Sometime later, hours or more, it seemed, she began to calm down and asked if she could continue her studies as it was the only thing she had left. Although somewhat reluctantly, she had been willing to continue participation.

CHAPTER THREE

Spector Walking the Library

Mother is gone! Walking the library is a specter pretending to be my Father, and I am the pseudo owner of this memory of my Grandfather's.

"What in blue blazes am I going to do with it?" Hansen continued to mumble while walking and staring around with new eyes. Until now, this home was a symbol of the family's history. Father was born here and so were my brothers. Grandfather built Aisling as a tribute to his love for Grandmother Nollaig and a desire to fulfill his bride's dream of freedom.

Both Grandmother and he were straight out of a Fred Astaire and Ginger Rogers movie. One of my favorite early childhood memories was watching the two of them. The strongest of these memories was when they danced in the ballroom. A five-piece band and singer would be filling the room with all the modern songs. With myself, my brothers and I outfitted in our finest. Robert, looking the most majestic, was naturally D'Artagnan, with Arthur playing the part of Arams and myself as Athos with our wolfhound playing Porthole's role. All the while, they, the three brave Musketeers, were bravely protecting the castle from the evil armies attempting to storm the walls.

As a child, I loved to hide and search in every nook, trying to find hidden treasures, even making up stories of Kings, Queens, and the Prince. And myself, of course, saving the Princess in a far off land, usually the treehouse in the great Elm tree in the backwoods past the patio and swimming pool. I would have to swim across rivers, climb mountains, and fight my way through the dark forest. Each time my heroic efforts saved the Princess played by a 12 pound cat named Cricket.

Grandfather created all this as a reflection of the dreams and hopes of a young man. He was a man smitten with the love of the Sea and a maiden who was needing saved. He named this place Aisling House, Irish for Dream House. I am now the new owner of a dream that is no more, even though it is still the Aisling House.

As the king of these three floors, huge basement, 21 rooms, 29 acres, gatehouse cottage, four employees, and the responsibility for all that plus my Father, I am genuinely the protector of the keep. I grew up in the history of this place. History that now is dissolving before my eyes and everyone else. Father is the last of that era. The dream that my Father duplicated of my grandfather's love affair with grandmother when meeting my mother.

She was a perfect replica of the stories I grew up with about my grandparents. Both of them were way ahead of the times. The sadness of these past generations of the lineage is now nearing its end. When Father passes, he will be the last with the name of Foireis. Thank the changing world that we no longer live in hostility because of a heritage that resulted in our need to change our surnames to a non-Irish name. Although I think I would enjoy our Irish name of Foireis a bit more than the name Folks.

His ruminations came to an end while a heavily burdened Hanson Folks turned back to the massive task at hand, that he was now the owner of this extensive estate. How this happened was initially outside of his comprehension. Father's ultimate dream was having all of his three sons become instrumental in the Foireis shipping empire created by his father Sinead. In turn, his father groomed first son Fredrick from, as some said, the day he left his mother's womb. His dreams flourished as Fredrick lived up to his every desire. So at the age of fifty-two, Sinead, in turn, inherited the same hopes for his boys.

Robert, the oldest son, not only avoided involvement with the business, he avoided most everything related to the ocean. The first time aboard the family's 110-foot yacht, five year old Robert became seasick. They had not reached the breakwater when Olivia begged Fredrick to turn *New Sea Breeze* about and cancel the outing.

Second son Arthur developed into a ship-shape seaman but dedicated himself to the study of biology. Prior to finishing the first twelve years of education, he received five different scholarship offers from prestigious universities for a Bachelor's in Biology placement. That left only the youngest son, who was accused of disgracing the Folks family and the Camoran's family.

Initially, Fredrick was pleased when Hanson married the daughter of the Camoran communication empire. He was also proud that Hanson applied for a Master's program in psychology. Fredrick believed his son would become an expert in personnel management, and even more so in negotiating for the Foireis shipping empire. By marrying the daughter of a communications empire, Hanson would be in position to continue their growing empire along with their daughter Barbara.

Then this son of his had the audacity to apply for a Doctoral degree by rejecting the tradition of joining the family business. Fredrick's disappointment was demonstrated by discontinuing his son's financial allowance, with a hope he would come to his senses. Instead, a son of his shamed himself and the Folks and Foireis names. He willingly became dependent on his new bride's financial allowance. His son became a freeloader.

Despite all of this, it was now becoming apparent the estate would be his. Within that tornado of craziness, at this moment, he needed to focus on the current issues. Hanson believed bringing Damon into the plan would help him to find clarity within this tornado. It will be even more essential if his Father's regression continues this obsession with spirituality. He even believes it will provide the answer for communicating with his departed wife Saoirse.

Damon might be able to formulate an answer and also provide a perfect opportunity for me. With his background and miraculous teaching abilities to connect with students, he may gain Father's attention, something that I have been unable to broach. The topic of Father's deteriorating physical and, emotional/mental health issues has been placed out of bounds. These issues are of the utmost priority, yet at the moment my hands are tied. Father refuses to address them and the rest of the family are deaf to them. Even the lawyers have backed off in relation to fathers behaviors. It appears his actions are not considered significantly abnormal enough to meet a level of behavior meriting a declaration of incompetency.

Additionally, the question of Yolanda's immediate state of mind certainly has become an intense concern in Damon's mind. Possibly, Damon himself might bring the topic to the table. He may suggest Yolanda could be helped by interacting with Father.

My brothers and the Folks Shipping Company lawyers have all been, to put it mildly, urging him to consider appointing someone as executor. The estate's employees, finances, and future needs would spiral out of control should physical illness, accident, or death occur to me. Damon may be the answer to a significant bundle of issues in one fell swoop.

CHAPTER FOUR

Where Did They Come From?

Sitting beside her bed at a loss of what to do, waiting for her to regain consciousness, Damon Soule, Doctor of Psychology, was helpless. Yolanda lay in the hospital bed and did not move, had not for over four days they said. The hospital staff had contacted him after finding his phone number in her wallet. He came immediately and was met by an individual that could be best described as a starched and creased.

Doctor Jameson MD began the discussion by adjusting his glasses, slightly tilting the head back and clearly talking down to Damon as if talking to a somewhat slow child. He started in a manner that suggested an investment in providing Dr. D a brief, simplified account of what led up to the patient's hospitalization.

"She had apparently been a participant in one of those disruptive group behaviors that required the National Guard to intervene." He stated in a manner indicating Damon might, in some way, be responsible,

"You know how those hippy types are? She had a Student Body card from that Marigold University! So what can you expect? No wonder she got knocked out." He looked down at the chart in his hand, paused, cleared his throat, and looking above Damon's head said,

"I mean no disrespect. It appears you are a Professor from that University. I must continue my rounds." Looking around, making eye contact with a nurse, said,

"Will you show," pause, looking back at the chart, "Professor, hmm, Soule to the patient's room." He then did a military about-face and departed.

The nurse with reddening cheeks identified herself as the charge nurse, then guided him down the hall and into an empty room, paused, then closed the door. Turned towards him and in a warm yet professional manner gave a detailed review of why they had called him and what the ambulance EMT explained had happened.

"Miss Swiftriver has an apparent trauma to the right side of her head, maybe a concussion. All her symptoms are inconclusive at this time. We just need to wait for her to regain consciousness. Until then, Dr. Jameson and, the medical team, have exhausted all the diagnostic data available."

Two days later, while sitting beside the bed, Damon began to reminisce about how this woman had modified his beliefs about the birth experience. These changes also impacted the direction of his research and his possible future as a Professor at Marigold University. All this and more began…

During the first Witchcraft class, Damon had noticed two engaging students, she sitting slightly forward, clearly intently interested, and he also keenly interested but in her not the course. So it was clear to Damon that these two students might be interested in volunteering for extra credit research participation. Her, because of apparent deep interest in the class's subject matter and the male student's apparent interest in researching her.

During the latter part of the next class, Damon outlined the benefits of participation in an extra credit research project. The female student Damon now knew as Ms. Swiftriver, was the first to sign the research roster, and her admirer Mr. Hawkins signed right behind her. Both students agreed to meet with him after next week's class.

He scheduled Swiftriver so Hawkins would not have "think" time to reconsider. Damon was willing to bet money the young man would be waiting around for Ms. Swiftriver to complete her interview. He was not as sure she would wait around for Mr. Hawkins to finish his. As Damon hoped, the young man did, and from that day forward the two always seemed together.

During the initial screening, both were scrutinized at a deep level. Next, in-depth testing for hypnotic susceptibility, the crucial go-no-go for appropriateness, was performed. Additionally, it was necessary to participate in a thorough personal history, primarily concerning early childhood.

Dean had been a willing enough subject, yet appeared guarded during his initial disclosures. Damon suspected childhood experiences were the explanation for this block. Somewhat reluctantly with gentle probing combined with relaxation training, he began disclosing that his grandparents had been strict religious fundamentalist. They had first condemned their unwed pregnant daughter, Dean's mother, then showed their Christian charity by adopting her bastard child. Dean had never been allowed to forget what his mother had done. This was also the reason his grandparents justified how they raised him.

He was not allowed to see his mother, not until her funeral. He was twelve and in the torment of puberty when informed of his "sinful mother's suicide." The first and only time he saw his mother was while she lay in a casket. For ignoring their order not to approach the coffin, he was required to complete two full months of penance. Only then did his grandparents see him fit to sit at their dinner table.

The young man had carried this imposed guilt into the present day. Damon acknowledged this as a confound related to Dean's deeply held resistance to dropping defense mechanisms. Because of this, it would strongly impact any openness to entering deep hypnotic states. Despite these confounds, he decided it would be worth taking a chance and decided to include his name in the list of available subjects.

Unresolved abandonment issues seemed to be one of the primary underlying connections between him and Yolanda. She, unlike Dean, seemed eager to explore her early childhood. The young lady's hypnotic susceptibility registered in the upper brackets of Damon's three-year-long research in this area.

In the first attempt to explore her susceptibility, she had fallen into a hypnotic trance almost instantaneously. Her initial screening and subsequent interviews indicated she was unaware of being exposed to hypnosis in her studies or any other part of her background. She acknowledged prior knowledge of the term hypnosis yet claimed no history of studying or experimenting in that field. This was most unusual with her incredible susceptibility to hypnotic suggestion.

Yolanda reported interest in psychology for investigating the origins of dreams and childhood development. She had also stated a keen interest in the historical accounts of witchcraft beginning in her early teens. Yet she had found it extremely hard to find critical scientific data on the reality and or the possibility of some accounts being factual.

Yolanda acknowledged it had been her primary motivation to sign up for Dr. Soule's Witchcraft class as one of her electives. It was also her hope that, at some level, the course would reflect similarities between witchcraft and Native American spirituality belief systems. This was her primary motivation for a desire to major in Sociology. In her initial interview, she indicated another strong interest to explore the spiritual belief systems outside of Christianity. She also wished to compare and contrast the two traditions.

She reported reading many articles on a new belief system termed Pagan Witchcraft and also Wicca. Most of what she discovered had, at least on a surface level seemed similar to what she had studied about Native beliefs. She did qualify this as depending on the authors, cultures, and religions. Even with this it seemed to her these beliefs were as valid as what was considered main-stream appropriate.

To Yolonda's why of thinking the majority of spiritual belief systems, of so called civilized cultures, tended to be cruel and repressive. It was also her opinion, a significant amount of the recognized studies identified as scientific also appeared to be hostile to beliefs outside of their own and consistently were described as cruel and repressive. Thus, it was her belief, this was an underlying causation for most warfare in current and ancient times.

Damon found himself becoming intrigued be this woman's myriad of interests. She also had what seemed an ability to interweave in and out of all these varied beliefs. His fascination became even stronger when she began participating in hypnotic regression during his experimental studies

During her third hypnotic trance, she reported experiencing what on the surface resembled past life memories. Based on these types of detailed experiences, Damon decided to place her in his deep regression studies and experiments. Dean once again followed her.

During the first deep regression, she reported faces that seemed to appear. She sensed they could be her parents. The faces had what she believed were Native characteristics. It was also her belief they were dark copper-colored people, with tears in their eyes staring down at her. They had long black hair like her own. The woman's eyes were possibly like hers and seemed to almost jump from her face. They were bright blue-green and enormous. She described the man's face as maybe her father's? His eyes were dark brown or black. Instead of jumping out, like the woman's, his seemed to pull at her. They were intense, as Yolanda looked into them. She described them as appearing to almost call her. Her mother's, on the other hand, seemed to come toward her. A lost baby deep down inside of her heart seemed to become active and wanting to reach out. When she sensed they were looking into hers or being looked at by these two sets of eyes, the adult in her was overwhelmed with a feeling of grief.

From that day forward, Yolanda did not doubt that her heritage was Native American. This helped explain her passion for gaining spiritual knowledge. She had not initially been aware of this aspect of her draw to Dr. Soule's class. She just knew that she was attracted to his witchcraft class. All this reinforced her never-ending thirst to find the truth of who she is. The experiences in Dr. Soule's regression study had just added more fuel to that fire.

Until the regression experiences, Yolanda had believed her last name was Swiftriver, as a result of being discovered as an abandoned baby, on a riverbank, at maybe two to three months old, no one knew for sure.

The discovery was close to a highway pull-off a hundred yards before a bridge crossed a swiftly flowing river. Yolanda's first foster home told her next foster parents there had been some evidence of suicide by a person that had left her at the river. The story continued from foster home to foster home up to and including her final foster home. This home was the closest Yolanda had ever cared to call her home. For four years, she lived with a couple not able to have children.

They requested that she refer to them as Mother and Father Posillico. It was the first time Yolanda had experienced how moderately wealthy people lived. It was also the first time she was provided with any material comforts. She knew that she was truly blessed. So over and over, she repeated, "Father Posillico, Mother Posillico. Over and over Father Posillico, Mother Posillico, Father

Posillico, Mother Posillico," no matter how hard she tried, it just never became comfortable.

It was a real joy to her that these strangers took her in. She believed that with everything they had, Mother Posillico, and Father Posillico tried to give her what she could ever want. Her history was just lacking something, maybe it was just a lack of ever having a "family," or maybe there was something broken in her, or perhaps she just did not know how to be loved. She had read about it, watched movies and TV shows, listened to music singing about love, but she was missing something and sure the hell did not know what.

The couple pretended more than actually loved her. Yet, the pretending led to being treated in a nurturing manner, perhaps like raising a dead relative's child more than their own child. Knowing they felt responsible for providing a good home for her. Paying her way through college and so many other "things," but no matter how much they gave, it wasn't able to fill the big void down deep in her belly.

So when she was accepted to Marigold University and left for school, the Posillico's behaved in a manner suggesting their job was completed. But they did pay for her college tuition, her room, and board, even provided her a significant allowance. On holidays, birthdays, and such, they would send a nice card and always money.

Yolanda did not blame them for not knowing how to love any more than she knew how to love them. They would always hold an exceptional place in her heart. She would try to access this place in her heart as a way to learn about close and loving relationships she had never experienced or known.

Based on what she had experienced with the Posillico's and what she was experiencing in the regression experiments, Yolanda thought she was finally finding some directions to follow. A path that would allow her to see so much more than what she had ever believed she was looking to find. Maybe she had a heritage? A name? And perhaps even a purpose.

Yolanda reported all this and more. Damon never doubted her sincerity in what she said, yet at the same time, he always had a doubt as to how much of what she reported was a subconscious desire for a heritage, and a answer to who she was?

CHAPTER FIVE

AWAKENING

Unaware that almost nine months had passed, Yolanda became aware of what might be something soft beneath her. Some unknown noise, and PAIN, some on her back, others on the side of her head. Needing to move! Tried to look around but could not see who was making noise. Knew it must be dark, pitch black dark.

Where was she, where in the hell! Afraid to speak and let them know she was here, she froze in place so they would not find her. But, but maybe she should, perhaps they were trying to rescue her. Staying as quiet as possible, she moved her hand, trying to feel what she was laying on.

"She's trying to come to," a voice called out and touched Yolanda's hand. Voices were all of a sudden all around her, and someone was touching her. She yanked back and demanded to know who was there. Instead, she only heard a crackly, hoarse sound coming from what felt like her mouth. More voices were surrounding her. She started struggling to sit up, was unable to. Her brain demanded to know what the hell was happening, but her mouth continued to make croaks and quacking sounds.

The overwhelming sound of voices, clanging, buzzing, banging, and beeping noises could not be understood. Where she was and why was she in a bed, no strapped in a bed. People were saying things in a language she did not know; they just spoke garble. She did not understand them and did not know how to ask something, she did not know. She just closed her eyes and fell back asleep.

Sometime later, she could hear them, but still not see them, there were people prodding poking and pulling on her. Now she could hear screaming. The first time this happened, she did not know who was screaming and shouting, then she knew it was her. She went away again to a place where she could see, yet seemed unable to talk. When viewing and wanting to talk, Owl seemed to hear what was in her mouth that could not speak.

The next time she awoke, she began to wonder why "they" made her blind? Or maybe they were keeping her where it was lightless? But then how could they see? Then she knew, and every time she became aware of being here, she knew that in this place, she was blind and began to cry.

Every day, every time, and anytime she was aware of, "whatever this hell was," she knew she could not see in this place. Then garbled sounds/language began to be filled with words that started to make sense somewhere deep inside her. It still seemed every time she tried to focus on the words! Sill nothing made sense.

Well, some of it she understood, some of the things they said to her such as water, or food, but it seemed to take a very long time. Was it days, hours, weeks?

Then she heard, "Can you hear me?" and "Can I get you something?" And the one question that seemed, like it was important to them, "Would you like to talk to *****" also took a long time to understand. It was a name that somewhere in her head seemed to be a word she knew. Yet it just didn't make sense.

Yolanda, no maybe YoYo, or perhaps the really nice Dances-as-Rain wanted to answer their questions but didn't know what they wanted her to say. Owl the "Seer-in-the-Dark" would understand and take the one called "Dances-as-Rain" flying, or sometimes to watch, but always teaching. Owl said Dances needed to allow herself to "see" and "hear" and "feel." Dances thought she was doing what was being asked. But she did not know how to do what was being asked. Sometimes it seemed Owl and those she could not see were both asking her to do the same thing, sometimes at the same time.

Owl told her that she did know how, she just needed to do. Dances thought Owl was trying to be funny, yet also knew Owl never would do that. So Dances just began to learn how to do. And she began to hear what she had not heard but knew she had.

This happened shortly after Owl had asked, "How did you see the elders and me at the fire?"

Dances was not sure what Owl was really asking, and asked, "Am I just dreaming you?"

Owl was an Owl, yet Dances knew Owl had smiled and then went away. Yolanda, Yoyo, and Dances was in a bed that was in a hospital with people doing, saying, and asking things that she did not know. "But what happened to Owl?"

In the other place, this place, they said they wanted to help, teach, and make things better. Nurses and others told her days, weeks, months passed, but she was unsure how long this was. Time was a thing she could not know.

Someone that she knew began to spend time with her. It was not Owl. She knew this because here in this place, she could not see. He that was talking, the one she knew, but had not known that she knew him until he told her.

He also told her she had been brought to Marigold Medical Center six months ago after the demonstration. He had been coming to see her at least once a week during that time. The more he spoke, the more she began to understand, she even began to know that she knew him and would soon remember something in the past about their past connections.

Doctors and nurses and others said they were here to help and came almost every day. They got her up from the bed and into a chair. At first, because she had been bedridden so long, she could not walk, and she even needed help to eat. Each day brought more information that she did not want and refused to believe, but was unable to change. She just wanted to go with Owl and never come back.

When Yolanda began to respond to the man she now knew as Dr. Soule, she began to remember who he was. He began to nudge her into participating at a higher level of personal effort in her rehabilitation. He encouraged her each time she became more self-sufficient.

Soon she was moving around the hospital room and adjacent areas. Dr. Soule sounded really excited when she began asking to eat at the hospital cafeteria instead of her room.

Even though she fought hard to follow instructions from both the hospital staff and the physical therapy techs, her blindness seemed to override her progress. By the end of each effort, she appeared to be drained of any motivation to continue. The positive steps forward tended to result in her tendency to regress into a deeper state of depression.

It slowly became evident the more she remembered of the past, precisely the demonstration and subsequent attack, the more she withdrew somewhere inside. At times it would only be five or ten minutes, but often, it was much longer.

Last week the withdrawal had been two hours short of two days, and when she awoke and called his name... instead of Dr. Soule somewhere deep inside asked for Dr. D. The sound of a gasp, and clatter of a chair scraping the floor told her that he was in the room, and a warm hand clasped hers, just as she demanded,

"What happened to Owl... Doc, what the hell happened? We were flying over the mountains; then I'm here. Why can't I see here? I see there, why not here. I don't want to be here, take me from this place, please, I'm begging, please."

CHAPTER SIX

Dr. D's Dilemma

As the days passed, Damon felt totally lost on how to help, but he didn't think he was as in the dark as the doctors. He and Yolanda had been intellectually involved for years. First, as Professor and student, researcher then research subject and finally as a pseudo-father figure. If he had to guess, given what he understood about her, it would be that she was more in-depth than he doubted any other person could imagine.

She has been the star volunteer research subject since that first class over six years ago titled Witchcraft/Shamanism, Psychological and Sociological Approach 342. She was the bright star in the classroom and even more so from the time she first volunteered for extra credit as a research subject. Every possible aspect of her behavior, intellect, and emotions analyzed as if under a microscope.

Yolanda's behaviors had followed a very consistent pattern for the first two years. Research for possible *in utero* memories that appeared to be approaching validation. To date, these were the most detailed memories that he was aware of, describing a pre-birth experience. Her information stayed consistent across eleven hypnotic regressions. This was strongly suggestive of a level of high validity.

Damon had enlisted two highly respected pediatricians willing to describe their experience, based on their professional practices. They reviewed the recording of Yolanda's descriptions as representative of the precise details they had experienced in their practice as pediatricians. Their stated assumptions were that

Yolanda was a highly educated and experienced pediatrician or possibly a mid-wife.

He was in the process of writing these findings for publication. Then the regressions took a decidedly unexpected direction. This change stopped him in his tracks. It resulted in a decision that the research needed shelving despite his desire to publish his findings.

During some of her hypnotic based regressions, especially the last three, she described people and places as if she was there. When she returned to the present, all the memories were still remembered. The last regression was designed to take place two days before that civil rights demonstration.

In the last regression study, after what seemed a very successful session, Damon decided it was time to begin bringing her from level three to level two, and was in the process of bringing her back up from level two into level one, when he snapped his fingers to finish the session. Instead of returning, both her words and behaviors indicated she was still in a hypnotic level three trance. She turned her head toward Damon and seemed to look him directly in the eyes, said his name, and started talking to the people in her trance. Damon felt his testicles tighten and shrink while his anus started puckering. Before he could respond, she smiled and said, "Sorry, I guess I forgot to return."

Then she turned and walked out the door. The next time Damon saw her was in the hospital. Luckily his phone number and address were in her wallet. He was the only one the authorities had been able to contact. Because of their history, Damon knew her better than anyone, except for maybe Dean. Nor was he even sure this was true.

Now she had four, maybe five, different doctors, all believing they had a handle on what Yolanda's diagnosis "should" be and what treatment regime was correct. Few of the professionals agreed with each other. It was unclear how many of them had attempted to consult with one another coherently. This and Dr. Soules's own beliefs gave him reasons to believe it was becoming imperative to get Yolanda out of this facility and somewhere that she might find comfort.

He was also aware that she needed a more organized treatment regime developed by a more cohesive medical team. Damon became convinced that he needed some outside professionals to work with her. Yet, he found himself fighting with himself against his own advice. What good would it do to convince other professionals to walk in here and develop different diagnoses and recommend different treatment plans?

The hospital's treatment team would be insulted. Furthermore, any professional from the outside might also be considered to be behaving in an unethical manner. That would only increase the conflicted environment that he was already observing. When he last met with the treatment team, there was talk about transferring her to a Psychiatric hospital for a possible commitment evaluation.

His attempts to intervene in the direction they were working towards was consistently met with irritation. Also, with arrogance, how dare you think a psychologist has a right to question our medical diagnosis. Dr. Jamseson, while in front of his team, even suggested that if Damon continued to disrupt the team meetings, he would be barred from them. And possibly even from visiting, for the patient's own good, of course.

At or near the explosion level, he attempted to walk out of the room in a dignified manner before giving them a basis to do what Jameson suggested. The only thing in his mind was, "I need to prevent this at all cost."

The next thing flooding his thoughts was analyzing all the consequences if she could not return to the study. Starting with my research there would be no one with even close to her ability to describe her regression experiences. And what about the idea of combining hypnosis with marijuana or… that LSD stuff. Then there is J.J. Lily's isolation tank, I haven't even discussed that idea with anybody. This thought stopped him in his tracks.

Oh my God! Even I forget her, and I'm the only one she has. It would be like she was being attacked all over again. Sometimes I act like a diagnostically self-center Narcissistic Personality Disorder.

Those idiots were talking about cold-induced hibernation, just a fancy name for ice-water baths. Plus electroshock therapy, and even combining this with drug therapy, specifically Thorazine. I even heard one of the psychiatrists mention a fucking lobotomy for God's sake, as if it was a joke. Well, it had to be, it's against the law. At least I think it is.

God, I have to get her out of this insane asylum before they put her in one. I was all wrapped around my ego, and she is in there alone, with an entire treatment team starting to recommend justifiable torture to do WHAT! Help her! If she has any chance, any at all to return to some level of sanity, I have to get her out of there!

With very little sleep, and what he might suggest as a new psychological diagnosis of tired brain syndrome, he returned to the hospital. To try one more time, to talk some sense into somebody. Find anybody that could possibly intervene in what was developing as far as this team of so-called experts.

Almost as soon as he stepped into Yolanda's ward, it seemed he was too late. The team was meeting to review her case. As he stepped into the room, the nurse was partway into describing what happened during the night shift,

"She went from being compliant to acting angry and resistant. This seemed to happen with no rhyme or reason. One moment she spoke calmly, and then in the mid-sentence, she was angry and verbally lashing out at me."

There was a moment of silence before Dr. Jamseson resumed,

"There is no doubt that the patient needs help. Not only rehabilitation for possible damage due to her brain trauma but also the unknown causes of these new behaviors. We clearly have not found any identifiable damage that's causing her inability to see. Her eyes show no pathology, yet she exhibits an inability to see. Yet, at the odd time, she denies she is always unable to see."

The staff psychiatrist went on reviewing his diagnosis of significant issues of brain trauma, which may be evidence of a disorder in intellectual functioning combined with minimal coping skills. As a result, he indicated prescribing valium until further diagnostic evaluations can be completed.

The neurologist suggested that because they had not been able to identify current physical damage, he considered exploratory brain surgery. Further, he still had not ruled out that a possible brain tumor might be causing these perceptions or hallucinations.

His statements made some sense concerning her reports of thinking she could see some where else, yet every indication was that she could not. It was also suggested there could be other factors that might be exacerbating and/or responsible for causing persisting perceptions. One possibility could be a result of using LSD and all that other stuff those demonstrator types might be on.

This was just one more voice condemning her, and it took all of Dr. Soule's emotional strength and fortitude not to punch the quack in the mouth. Instead, he clamped his lips, turned his back, departed the ward, and chose to call a colleague that he had worked with for years and, on occasion, asked for a second opinion.

After a fast-paced walk around the hospital grounds and a lot of deep breathing, a plan started to form. First, he needed to phone Dr. Zoie Philmore, the colleague he had been thinking of. She had a background not only in stress disorders but also in several cases diagnosed with repressed trauma.

Zoie was not just a colleague. She was, well, someone who

made his world less lonely, a lot less alone if he was going to be totally completely truthful. He had been discussing Yolanda's case with her and until recently had not considered asking her to step in and examine Yolanda. Zoie could also have knowledge of a more therapeutic environment to relocate her.

He left the hospital and took a cab back to Maggie U. Back in his office, he began reviewing what he knew. What the medical staff thought they knew and what he hoped Zoie could help accomplish with his help. Deep in thought concerning the way Yolanda talked about that strange place with an owl and people looking at her, he decided to discuss it with Zoie. Then the phone rang, Hanson Folks was on the other line. Before the conversation ended Damon began developing a plan.

This might be the perfect chance to help her. Hanson may even suggest it himself. It would meet all our hopes, and Yolanda knows the Aisling House, and everyone there loved her.

PART THREE

CHAPTER ONE

Leaving the Hospital

By the time Dr. D left to meet Hanson, Yolanda was ready to pack up and go, while quietly saying to herself,

Dr. D's half assed afterthought attempt to inject caution into the discussion, is not OK! It's about me getting out of this hell hole. His so-called idea of caution was completely lost on me. Caution was not something she could grasp with all the desire to run, feeding her urge to climb into her wheelchair and head for the door. This urge lead to a not so quiet, "His suggestion of moving me to Aisling House and then attempting to change that idea too, well to say the least, is just a bunch of BS."

His statement of, "I just had an idea and wanted to explore your thoughts on it," That too was a load of BS. What does he think I am! I might be blind but I sure as hell am not stupid! He had to know this whole line of crap was not something I would swallow.

When I heard the words suggesting I had a chance of getting out of "Here!" made my heart jump with a shout of yes, yes, yes! Minutes later, angst kicked in with no! NO! No... What is out there? Are They! going to attack me again? How do I manage being blind out there? Who's going to be my guide, cook, caretaker, and all the other things I need.

"We need to measure your vital signs" broke into her emotional flooding, and her vital signs took another jump.

"Why in the hell can't they at least announce themselves?" She asked herself and this unknown nurse, LPN, or some other somebody.

"Well, Dear, we have to check vitals every hour. It is the policy, you know," Yolanda heard a voice state.

Damn, I must have said that out loud, God, I have to get out of here. I can't take any more. I don't need therapy. I need sanity! She moaned inside her head.

Having become quite adept at just tuning out and going inside, she let herself begin to fade out. Hoping Owl might be waiting, telling herself to tune back in and become present when Zoie came into the room. It shouldn't be long now.

Memories of the first time she saw Aisling House, took her away. Her first view of the estate triggered feelings of awe as she watched the large gates swing open. It was the first time she had an experience of seeing powered gates opening themselves. Dr. D. punched a code into a box and bingo the gates swing open. Then they were passing a large home with ivy covering the brick walls on one side. It was like a large cottage in a never-never land picture. She remembered thinking this would be like living in a fairytale. The thought lasted but a moment as they drove past the home. Dr. D just kept driving while explaining it was where the Caretaker Albie and his family resided.

It seemed like ten maybe even fifteen minutes that they continued along the tree-lined roadway—then rounding a curve in the road, a building that would shame some small hotels, perhaps even some midsize ones, came into view. Feelings of awe began to overwhelm Yolanda. It was unbelievable and could not come close to anything she had ever actually seen. Not even movies would be able to mimic the experience. The experience became even more unbelievable as they approached.

Yolanda knew this would be a moment she would always remember.

Disbelief and, at the same instant, a sensation of being transported to another time and place. Willies began overwhelming her as they drove up to this castle-like mansion thing that seemed hundreds of years old.

Dr. D told her his motive to visit Aisling House developed shortly after she and Dean went down different paths. That was when she had lost her drive, both academically and socially. How her participation in the research project became haphazard. She remembered how he continually attempted to find ways to give her higher praise than she deserved. She knew he was trying to motivate some encouragement in her. She had lost the emotional sparkle that drove her research participation and could not re-kindle it. Yet Dr. D continued suggesting and, in this case, openly encouraged her to find renewed motivations.

He had strongly spoke of how this could become an outstanding opportunity for her to re-engage in her doctoral thesis research. Then he began describing the Aisling House library as one of the most extensive Parapsychological collections in the United States and emphasizing that it ranked in the top ten in the world. Yolanda's interest moved from somewhat curious to full-on excitement at this point.

As her enthusiasm began to show, she remembered Dr. D's saying his trepidation was also beginning to decrease, telling her he had watched his research project move from a Kentucky Derby contender to a plodding packhorse, when she and Dean separated, and how crushing it seemed for all of them. Now the true gift was watching her intellectual energy renewing along with her desire to learn and that beautiful sparkle in her eyes was making a come back. It was, according to him, a new beginning happening. He believed she now had the opportunity to immerse herself in the Aisling's Library, saying…

"I believe this could be an incredible opportunity for your emotional life and motivation to return." He followed this by admitting his underlying hope wast that it would restore a desire for completing her Doctoral Thesis. This disclosure energized him to become openly honest with my own research needs. "If all this comes true, you might be persuaded to believe coming to Aisling House was the best thing that could happen."

Dr. D. went on describing how he remembered watching as her relationship with Dean developed and became deeply serious. Sadly as this happened it resulted in her Doctoral Thesis taking a backseat. On the other side of the coin, their participation and talents gave the regression project an incredible boost to a higher level of outcome validity. When Dean disappeared, her investment dropped toward the floor. She was also well aware that Dr. D's research project reliability studies also fell.

Dr. D continued to discuss her Thesis project and how the Aisling's Library could provide collaborative validation. As her awareness of these possible new avenues for exploration grew, the more her enthusiasm seemed to increase. That was the beginning of an increasing desire to return to possible participation in his research, as all the pieces appeared to be falling into place. Her enthusiasm increased his enthusiasm and excitement leading to a belief in the possibility that the research might start anew. Then with a slight pause of pleasure and hope, as he continued his tour guide dissertation on Aisling House's history with,

"Fredrick's Grandfather built this a little over ninety years ago."

What seemed like a fairytale fantasy flooded Yolanda's thoughts as Dr. D continued his guided tour presentation,

His Grandfather met Grandmother Nollaig in Savannah Georgia when his ship *Breeze Farraige*, which is Irish for *Sea Breeze*, needed reconditioning before the next voyage. Grandmother, at that time, was an indentured servant for a wealthy family. The family lived in a mansion in an area that only the upper crust of Savanna resided.

Grandfather built Aisling House as a copy of that mansion as a reminder of how he had met his only Love. He swore she would always live in a home that she would be proud to call her own and for the rest of her life, walk through the front door, knowing she would never be anyone's servant again. She would be the Mistress of her home. It would be a home that displayed his Love for her," Dr. D's voice and demeanor indicated deep emotion as he continued,

"The first time I met his family was when Hanson invited me to a graduation party in honor of his brother Arthur's eldest daughter. I want to emphasize that I felt totally out of place in such a distinguished group of people. It was an environment I could only imagine. Pardon me, because I need to change that to a situation I could not even imagine.

Hanson introduced me to his brothers then later, his Father. A sensation of being overwhelmed was just a beginning. Next, he proceeded to walk me into what he said was the Library. In the middle was a huge leather couch. An elderly gentleman stood up from it and said,

So this is that protege you speak so highly about, please introduce me. Guess it is your turn to give to another, what Professor Grayson gave to you, all those years ago.

I nearly wet myself and, at the same time, attempted to carry on a conversation. In front of me stood the owner of a vast shipping empire and the wealthiest man I had ever personally seen, let alone met. Now I was standing in his home, with my mind attempting to understand when he said, he knew who I was. Professor Hanson Folks had talked to this man and others about me. Me!, as his protégé

Not much else stayed in my head, not what he said or I said. The next clear memory of that day was his brother, Arthur, a highly respected scientist and the father of two daughters. I fell in Love with his youngest, let me change that to…Fell, head over heels in Love, with EmmaRay, Who I married a bit over six months later. To this day, I believe we had been a perfect picture marriage until she and my two young children went shopping. They never returned. A huge truck, driver asleep at the wheel, hit them head-on."

Dr. D slowed the car to a stop, turned to Yolanda, tears in his eyes, with a desolate sob, in an almost silent whisper said, "It was a closed casket funeral for all three."

They sat quietly for a long spell. Opening the door, Dr. D stepped out and loudly blew his nose. He reentered the car, started the engine, and continued to drive toward the grand entrance of Aisling House. When they arrived, he once more exited the vehicle, walked around the front, and opened her door, saying, "Shall we," then led her up the nine marble steps to what must have been at least 12 foot-tall magnificent double doors and clapped the clapper.

The grandeur was truly overpowering yet did not seem to quell a deep, almost smothering loneliness reaching out from the vast structure. It was like it had been abandoned and was just waiting, waiting for something, something that Yolanda was unable to describe. One of the large mahogany doors swung open, as she wondered how Dr. Folks and Dr. D could refer to this as a home.

Instead of Dr. Folks answering the door a fifty-something woman with a brilliant smile stepped forward and while hugging Dr. D, locked eyes with Yolanda and said,

"This must be that young Lady you keep raving about? I'm Mrs. Holbert the housekeeper." Then stepping closer, clasped Yolanda's hand and said,

"I have waited quite some time to meet you, my dear. Please come in." Stepping farther inside and gently pulling Yolanda with her, she called out, "Hanson, they have arrived."

Feeling astounded would be mild for what was happening to Yolanda's understanding of the word 'wealthy.' The entranceway was much larger than her apartment. Sure her apartment was a studio, but this was… Oh my God, the ceiling was twenty or maybe even thirty feet high. For the next thirty or forty minutes, if asked, she would say she was speechless. To describe the impact on her emotions and mind would be impossible. This entire experience was beyond her understanding, yet these people were behaving as if it was a home.

All of this changed the moment she stepped through the Library double doors and entered. It was like she was Eliza Doolittle walking into the library/study portrayed in the movie *My Fair Lady*. Feeling as giddy as a little girl, waking up to the grandest Christmas morning with gifts everywhere. All she wanted was to touch and look at every book on each shelf. For a short time, her life began to move from being black and white to glorious technicolor. She became excited with thoughts about her Thesis and even about resuming participation in Dr. D's regression studies.

Things such as the interrelationships between susceptibility, mysticism, and religion whisked her intellect into multiple directions. Each was suggesting unseen discoveries that would open doors to understanding the unknown. If only she could absorb all that was before her. Mr. Fredrick Folks' Library took her into the center of a whirlwind of information.

Shelves reaching the ceilings, row on rows seemed to fill the space. Down the center of the room were several overstuffed comfortable leather easy chairs, small tables, a long table with four wooden chairs and nooks and crannies here and there. As they neared the end of the center aisle, Yolanda heard what sounded like a low muttering seemly coming from behind the last set of shelves. Stepping past the one on their right, she saw a wild-haired balding and stoop-shouldered man muttering to the book in his hands.

"Let me introduce you to my father," Professor Folks said quietly as if not to disturb the muttering man.

"He is the crucial reason I have invited you and Damon here to the Library. My father has spent the last year in this room, seldom leaving except for, ah, personal needs. He is searching for a way to find my mother."

"Time to take your vitals," a nurse's voice broke the silence, and Yolanda was back in the present. The loss of Dean, her feelings about civil rights, and the developing Vietnam conflict all had faded for a moment in time. But now she was back, back in this hospital and all it meant.

All she had lost, not just her eyesight but so much of her life, what it had been and now how blind it was. The incredible Library she would never be able to see. Now it seemed she might have a chance to return to that lonely castle on the hill. But for what?

Catching her breath, she attempted to accept what would be an incredible gift just to get out of this, this place. Maybe one day she would write a story. It would be about a place that seemed to be dedicated to not helping people become healthy but to run them through a human repair garage that would remove and replace broken parts and give tune-ups. A place that could not or would not have any respect for the love and devotion a human body needs. The medical world did not seem to understand that healing must be about all four aspects of humanness intellectual, emotional, spiritual, and physical for true healing to occur. Without this, it was like attempting the creation of a Beethoven symphony only using three flutes.

Tears began to flow and sobs burst from her chest, her mind screaming, "You are Fucking! Blind! And you are going to do what?" Somewhere in this morass of grief, she fell asleep, a sleep of exhaustion and pure panic a sleep that could be easily confused with a coma.

CHAPTER TWO

Back to Maggie U

The butt-end of the new Corvette started to slide. He slammed the gas pedal to the floor, the powerful engine screamed, tires clawed the road, and the car catapulted out of the curve. The nose of the Corvette straightened out just as Dean tossed a silky, yet lightning fast shift to fourth gear. A satisfied grin cracked his firmly set lips as he settled in for the next curve.

I'm back, he thought, breaking into a full-face smile and clearing the next curve. Highway 101 stretched out before him in as straight a line as its snaky route would allow. Dean relaxed and let himself think about being back. Now he was driving down a road leading to what he hoped would be a reunion with Yolanda.

Like Paul, she was someone else that he had not heard or been able to understand what she was seeing. He had seldom let himself think about her while in Far East Asia. It was too confusing and emotionally painful.

Now on his way back to a time before, a time of believing, loving, and innocence, he began remembering, the time he had been studying a list of available classes. He heard some girls sitting at a table next to his, talking about a "Dr. D" and his new course on Witchcraft.

"What the hell," he thought, swiveling his head in their direction to see who was dumb enough to get excited about a Witchcraft class. That swivel and the incredible green eyes that were looking directly into his pushed, against his better judgment. By the end of the day, he somehow signed up for *Witchcraft/Shamanism, a Psychological Approach 342*, as one of his elective classes.

During the next three days, he had actively worked to convince himself the class was going to be interesting. This belief continued right up to the day and time he needed to enter the classroom. While walking down the corridor to the class, he decided to keep walking past the room. He didn't need some dumb ass class like... When emerging from around a corner, those green eyes met his, and her voice said,

"The classroom is this way. You must have missed it."

A full hour later, he began gathering his books, watching her, and wondering what the class would entail. One thing he did know was he needed a way to meet Green Eyes. Dean became lost in the chaos of other students grabbing books, talking, and walking toward the door. He had lost her of the green eyes. In a low-level panic, Dean began swiveling his head around, trying to catch sight of her. While looking behind and up into the raised seating, he somehow "accidentally" bumped into her. One more time, Green Eyes was staring into his, and all he could do was mumble an "Oh…sorry."

"Oh really, hmmm, and I thought you might have been trying to get my attention" the mouth, the perfect mouth replied as the lips began to smile.

"So, what is your name, and did I notice you staring at me most of the class, or was it my imagination?" Then she turned and started walking, asking…

"Well, are you coming?"

Within days she had his heart, and he hers. For almost two years, the heavens smiled on him. The two were seldom ever seen far from one another. They signed up for the same classes, and both declared a major in psychology. They also volunteered for the same extra credit research related to psychology or social psychology.

Dr. Damon Soule became their advisors and recruited the pair for his early childhood regression studies. It seemed the perfect romance for the two and ideal for Dr. Soule's research program until the world turned upside down.

"Vietnam happened."

Yolanda became a Dove and began actively participating in demonstrations both against the war and for civil rights. Dean, on the other hand, became a Hawk supporting the war and refused to participate in protests. He had believed at that time he had some, well ok not a ton of understanding. Well, maybe some around her demonstrating for civil rights, but he found no acceptance for her stand against the war. Opinions so profoundly felt that tore their relations apart.

He could not contain his Hawk viewpoint when she began demonstrating against the war. He felt she was personally attacking the men fighting for their country. She thought he was supporting them dying for nothing. Dean then made a decision that changed any chance of continuing the relationship.

He believed it would also back up his viewpoint when deciding to join the Navy. Yolanda backed her views by becoming a driving force in the war against the war. They never found a way to communicate with each other after that. Now the only thing he could understand was his need to apologize to her the same way he had to Paul.

The phone call while at the Chevrolet dealership helped him make a decision. Not only did Dr. Soule answer the phone, but he sounded excited Dean was back. It wasn't until Dr. Soule mentioned Yolanda was still assisting him on a research project that Dean made up his mind about what to do.

He was going to see, well he hoped to see, YoYo. Somehow calling her Yolanda seemed way too formal. His pet name YoYo was different. It was connected directly to the day he knew he was in love.

They had been in bed, sweaty and still breathing hard when his mouth said YoYo I think I'm falling for you, during the long pause, she quietly whispered in his ear,

"Me too."

From that day forward, her name was YoYo to him. Now he had to find out if she would see him. Then he might have some idea of what to do with his new life.

Another serpent of turns loomed ahead for challenging his driving skills. For another day, he just drove. A day later, he was walking down a deserted, still, familiar corridor, with echoes following his footsteps, at Marigold University or as it was fondly and by some not so fondly called Maggie U. It still looked and almost felt like it had been yesterday when the fight had taken place in this very corridor. They were leaving Dr. Soule's class, Historical Approach to Psychology, the final class of his undergraduate career.

YoYo had not been involved with or even verbalized an interest in Vietnam when they met. She did participate in supporting civil rights and seemed to have a deep emotional connection to the movement. Dean had some intellectual interest in civil rights and encouraged her.

He devoted his energy to philosophy and specifically the underlying philosophical principals of Christian based religions. Two months before the completion of their B.S. Degrees, it became evident she was also becoming a card-carrying dove concerning the Vietnam conflict.

The arguments began when Dean was siding toward the Hawk viewpoint of the Vietnam war issue. He had attempted to keep his opinions out of their relationship, but it had not worked. It was like they were playing out the same controversy that was filling the current news both in the newspapers, television news and on campus.

Before meeting YoYo, he had an iron-clad commitment, not to date psych majors. That also had not worked, and now he was on the way back to hopefully rectify that mistake. Their relationship had been the first time he thought he knew how it felt to experience love. Then when she began participating in the demonstrations, instead of working to understand, he ran.

Dean still clearly, did not understand the rights and wrongs of this particular war. Nor why he was standing in front of Dr. D's office door trying to pretend it was Dr. Soule he wanted to see. Instead of a beautiful black-haired psychologist named Yolanda.

He just stood there in front of the door, hand sweating and staring at the nameplate for a very long time. One last time he glanced up at the plate;

Damon Soule BS, MS, PhD

Professor of Psychology

Office Hours

2:00 PM to 4:30 PM Wed - Fri

CHAPTER THREE

Dr. D and Dean

The door snapped open just as Dean reached up to knock. His knuckles came within an inch of rapping the most memorable man he had ever met, right in the forehead. Dr. Soule's five-foot eight-inch stature would typically be short for Dean's six-foot two-inch frame, yet the power that radiated from the man, made Dean feel like the smaller man.

The first time Dean saw Dr. Soule, he was working out at the gym. Dean remembered wondering what a theatrical type, like that, would want in the gym??? Then thinking maybe another man. Dr. Soule disappeared into the dressing room, and Dean continued doing inclined sit-ups.

An hour or two later, Dean decided to play some racquetball and ran into Dr. Soule looking for someone interested in playing a few sets. Dean considered himself in the upper echelon of players, at least at the college level, so was not too excited about playing with this short caricature of a Professor. Within an hour, Dean found his athletic ego shattered and humbly thanked Dr. Damon Soule for the games. If he was truthful it was actually thanking him for the lesson in ego destruction and wondering at the same time who that masked man was.

Now all these years later, Dr. Soule's piercing black eyes were boring into his, and his booming voice was inviting him to come in and sit down. Dr. Soule, with distinct pleasure, began telling Dean he would cancel his afternoon appointments as he was picking up the phone.

Dean moved toward a chair and sat down feeling some trepidation mixed in with the excitement of hoping Dr. D would lead him to YoYo. Then thought, damn, I might not have that right, maybe instead I should call her Yolanda? She and Dr. D might think I am the outsider and then what am I to say; that's when Dr. Soule's voice broke into Dean's thoughts.

"So son, you are back, and I want to hear what brought you back to good old Maggie U?" While trying to think of a response he also paused for a moment becoming aware Dr. Soule hadn't changed since Dean had seen him last. The same eyebrows, goatee, and slicked-back hair. Just as he began refocusing on Dr. D's question, the phone rang again, Dr. D answered and began a conversation. Dean quietly sighed with relief and sat back in the chair glad he had a moment to find an appropriate answer to the question Dr.D asked. The moment was not nearly long enough before he heard,

"Well, son, it's been a long time. What's on your mind? Guess you are wondering about Yolanda?" Dr. Soule said, hanging up the phone, and leaning back and packing his pipe. As usual, Dr. Soule didn't waste time on small talk. Dean still felt uncomfortable with the man's directness. Also, with his uncanny ability to know what was on Dean's mind.

Dean attempted to talk about Nam as if his primary interest was Dr. Soule instead of YoYo. By the third sentence, Dr. Soule interrupted him and started to talk about his research and Yolanda's participation in it. Dean was much more interested in how to contact her, then what she had been doing.

Dr. Soule continued telling Dean about the research. Dean kept listening for clues as to her whereabouts. Without even knowing he was being asked, Dean was soon volunteering to resume working with Dr. D and YoYo. Their research sounded similar to what he had first became involved in before joining the Navy. Back then, it was something that seemed slightly silly to him. YoYo's participation was the hook that pulled him in, just like today. Dean remembered not being impressed when she first mentioned working with Dr. D in some regression type studies. Dr. D is now indicating she is instrumental in a significant research project that grew from the original experiment.

He remembered how the class *Witchcraft, a Psychological and Sociological Approach 342*, introduced him to Yolanda Swiftriver. It felt almost like yesterday when he had tried to convince himself of taking the course because of an interest in how witchcraft influenced both past cultures and modern-day religions. Even then, he knew he followed her into that class, not because of an interest in the topic but an interest in her. Consequently, he developed an interest in the topic, Dr. D, and any way to be with YoYo.

Even to this day, Dean was still unsure why YoYo affected him the way she did. He had to admit physical attraction had a lot to do with it, at first anyway. After all, with her looks and build, it was hard not to notice her presence. She was one of the few women he could almost look eye directly to eye. At five foot ten plus, if she wore heels, she was maybe an inch shorter than him.

Remembering how he noticed her radiant black hair and sparkling green eyes the first time he had seen her. A woman looks were not something that generally made him go against his better judgment. Nor were Psych majors interested in the mystical and spiritual on his radar. But when it came to YoYo, these things just didn't seem to matter. By the fourth day of class, they became inseparable. They remained that way right up to the big blow up. Now he was back. The United States felt and looked like a different country. He felt ashamed of his part in the war. YoYo, on the other hand, had given up demonstrations and political activism for full-time participation in research. According to Dr. Soule, she had completed her Ph.D. and was still not working unless she considered this research thing work. According to Dr. Soule, she had become quite the noted expert in how susceptibility and the mystical were the underpinnings of religions.

As he listened to Dr. D, he began to think YoYo's total engrossment in these beliefs might be just what he needed. Raised in a strict Baptist foster family, he had carried strong convictions into Vietnam combat, which his religious background had not prepared him for. At first, the behaviors of his shipmates had shocked him. Then he found himself embracing the same actions. Now he felt embarrassed and ashamed.

YoYo and Dr. D were the only connections he had left in this land that now felt foreign to him, a nation that had been his country when he had left it four years ago. During his initial military training and flight school, he was living in a world of ponytails, lowered cars, and rock and roll. The glory of the Kennedy administration was terminated when the president was assassinated. A year later, he left for Vietnam. Now he was in the land of Hippies, miniskirts and the Beatles. He did not have any family connections. His dad, actually his grandfather, had disappeared, and the woman that wanted him to call her mother was dead. Now he hoped that YoYo could help him reconnect to the strange country that he had returned to.

Dean had been pretty insecure when he finally developed enough courage to ask Dr. D for YoYo's phone number. There was no way for him to know how she would respond by him contacting her. When they had broken up, it had felt permanent. It was as if they had lost all the things he had believed they had in common. Now he was confused about what he thought and what he didn't.

He began to reveal this confusion with the hope Dr. D would help him. Instead, the excellent Doctor started describing what had been happening to Yolanda. When Dr.D had finished, Dean had heard about the demonstrations, tear gas, and students shot by the National Guard. Added on top was Yolanda blind and hospitalized for almost nine months.

To say he was stunned would be a significant understatement. All this was all too much, almost getting him back in his Corvette and running like hell. Dean believed he had enough confusion and change, and then Dr. D said the one thing that brought him back,

"Yolanda needs your help, son. I have run out of ways to help. So far, Yolanda has listened to our idea, but to be truthful has been very hesitant to participate. An associate of mine, Dr. Zoie Philmore, and I have one other thought.

First, I need to bring you up to date of what transpired after you enlisted in the military. Yolanda was devastated and totally lost. Please understand what I am going to say is just my hypothesis about how your departure may have led to her emotional collapse.

Yolanda was abandoned by what I suspect was her mother. She was less than seven months old when found by that river. She was then moved from foster care to foster care until the Posillico couple took her in. They could never have a child of their own. I suspect their willingness to adopt Yolanda was something of a mid-life crisis decision, and a well-intentioned gesture. The underlying issue was that they were attempting to fulfill a profound dream that would never come true. The result was that they were trying to use Yolanda to fill that void.

They were unable to experience the heartfelt love of authentic parenting with a child, not of their own. They gave her things, trying to make them the same as love. The incredible sadness of this situation was two people working on loving one seven-year-old, one desperately needing love, while the truth was neither they nor Yolanda knew how.

When you and she parted, Yolanda did not have the ego strength or defense mechanisms to deal with the ending of your relationship. My opinion and please hear it is just my opinion, the two of you experienced the closest either of you ever came to being loved and loving another.

You gained acceptance and purpose in the military. Also, a very effective escape mechanism of discounting your emotionality. Emotionality that if I understand correctly is not encouraged to be discussed, displayed, or accepted as part of the military or most jobs.

Your job was to not feel, in let's say a vulnerable way. My assumption is that you put all your energy into what the mission called for. I might even go out on a limb, and guess that you stayed physically exhausted.

You seldom had a good night's sleep and orchestrated each day so there was minimal opportunity for self-reflection and or emotions.

Now I want to describe Yolanda's side of this picture, Not long after you left, Professor Folks' mother passed away. His father was unable to resolve the loss of his cherished partner, wife, and confidant. His inability to accept this loss became much more evident as being a recluse became his refuge. This powerful baron of a shipping empire gave up everything and spent most of his day and night mourning his loss.

Professor Folks and I began encouraging Yolanda to take a sabbatical at Aisling House as a guest. The real purpose behind this encouragement was to entice Yolanda to help Hanson's father Fredrick and therein herself. If she was face to face with the level of mourning, she might begin to find a way out of her own morass." He then went on to describe what had unfolded as per Yolanda's descriptions.

By the time Dr. D had finished with Yolanda's story, Dean was reconsidering what to do. Before he had a chance to make a decision, Dr. D cleared his throat and continued by describing how his wife and children died, what it had been like and how lost he had been. Finally, silence fell heavy on the room as both Dean and Dr. Soule with tears in their eyes sat staring at nothing. When Dean found the courage to look up and saw tears start to run down Dr. D's cheeks, he knew he could not leave.

He had only met Dr. D's wife one time at a picnic. He and his wife had invited Dean and Yolanda to attend. Yolanda fell in love with Dr. D's wife, or more likely with their little five-year-old son. They only had one child at the time, but it was evident his wife was pregnant with their next child. He began to speak, when he was cut off in mid sentence as Dr. D continued as if he was unaware Dean was talking.

"Two months later, the school year was over, and your relationship with Yolanda's was at an end. You were on the way to Aviation Officer

Candidate School." Dr. D's last statement with tears running down his cheeks,

"I haven't even told Yolanda this, but the two of you became my surrogate kids. Retroactive for sure, but Yolanda was here, and I pretended her brother Dean was in Vietnam. I just don't have the words to tell you how happy I am that you are back, I wish I could tell you the same for Yolanda, but that will be up to her. Please know I need your help, but more importantly, she needs your help."

Dean was thunderstruck by Dr. Soule's torrent of not just information but deep emotions of pain and loss. Emotions that flowed forth for the last hour plus. Dean thought he was the one who would acknowledge how insecure and just plain scared he was before entering Dr. D's office. Now he wasn't just astonished; he was feeling like ropes were tied around all of his emotions and pulling in ten different directions. He was feeling pain, fear, pity, sadness, and a wealth of others for himself, for Dr. D, for Paul Simpson, for Yolanda.

He was choking back tears, snot starting to run from his nose, and a great big massive rock grew in his throat. He blubbered a croak and a horse thank you. He started to move toward Dr. D to hug, but pulled back and stammered something, but didn't know what and bolted from the room. With tears blinding him and a swirling brain that did not know where to go, he found the Corvette, and cried until…

Damon sat at his desk, then sat some more, A blank brain was the only thing he knew. An hour or maybe two later, he left his office and then returned without sitting down, reached for the phone and called Zoie.

Leaving his office he was thinking about how Dean's return might affect both the research, and more importantly, YoYo's recovery. The wavering emotional stability began returning, knowing he would lose all of his composure with all the emotional strength he had left and began to push back his feelings. He was unsure if Dean's return would be positive or negative, but he did know it would change his future, both as a Professor and as a researcher. Yolanda and Dean had been a pivotal team in changing the direction, depth, and result of his research. If they became reunited maybe it could reestablish the validity of his study, Dr. D mused on his way to meet Zoie for a dinner date.

During the drive to pick up Zoie, he could not stop thinking about Yolanda's past research issues. The starting point was reviewing how in a despondent state she began struggling to attend classes then came to him wanting to withdraw from school. Her research participation had became haphazard, so different from her past behaviors in intensive projects that took deep and consistent concentration.

It was apparent she and Dean had reached a significant impasse. Dean also had disappeared from classes, so even when she was present, she was not. Now the project they had all envisioned might come to a whimpering end. A project that would have a profound impact on how the effect of the in-womb experience impacts personality development.

Dean's returning had a possibility of bringing the two back together. Damon and the two of them could become forever entwined in the literature identifying his research as proof of pre-birth memories. Yolanda and Dean were the bright burning stars in that research and would be critical to its possible success. If this did not happen, all of this, from day to day, was sliding into non-significance.

Damon's career and even his reputation could be, and probably would be directly correlated to this outcome. If he could not resurrect at least Yolanda's full participation, the study would most likely fade to the dusty archives of failed/unfinished research. The only thing he could think had a chance of relighting the flame was Yolanda's escape from the hospital. If only there were a way to re-engage her interest in the information she had sought out and continuously tried to understand. Aisling House possibly could be the catalyst that could do that. It had to do it. Believing this to be the key, Damon knew Dr. Hanson Folks was the one with the key. And literally, the key was in his pocket.

His mind was running in circles around his brain. He wanted to call Zoie, but also Hanson Folks, rescue Yolanda and find what the hell happened to Dean. All of them fought him for acknowledgment. But the number one question was what about Dean, did I scare him away? Is he going to try to and see Yolanda?

CHAPTER FOUR

CAW

Dean felt the tears begin to build, wanted to stop, but at the same time did not. He remembered running, sort of, scared and running from? It was Damon. No, it was him. No, it was?? Where in the hell am I, and how long have I been driving? He looked down at the gas gauge, a little over a quarter of a tank. Damn this could be the shits.

He slammed on the brakes, tires squealing as they locked up, the Corvette came to a sliding stop. Dean looked around trying to focus, and all he saw was darkness and the headlights showing trees, big trees crowding both sides of the road. He was not sure where he was or why he slammed on the brakes. He had to piss, so maybe that was why the road appeared deserted. Yet he was unsure, remembering a way back that might have been a road leading into the woods.

Tossing the four-speed into reverse, he backed up until he could see the dirt road leading into the trees. Spinning the steering wheel, he eased the Vette into the woods, if for no other reason than to relieve his bladder. At the most a hundred, hundred fifty feet of what he thought was a road disappearing into the brush. Still, it was off the road and a place to park.

Stretching legs and aching back, then just standing beside the Corvette, he let his stream flow as he looked around. The headlights were showing some long ago tire tracks that continued into the woods. Job completed, he zipped up, and decided it was time to begin inspecting what might provide an interesting place to explore for at least a night's rest.

Climbing back into the driver's seat, he began easing the car forward. The clangs and bangs as the car bottomed out in chuckholes and ruts suggested he needed to find a pullover soon. Off-roading was not part of the Vette's personality. As if the cosmos heard his need a few minutes later, a small clearing off to the side of the tracks indicated possibilities. So he angled the car towards the clearing, the headlights illuminated what looked to be a resting spot.

Luckily the day before or maybe the day before that he had stopped in a four-block village with a cafe. The breakfast was steaming hot, covered the entire plate, and could feed two hungry men. His hunger satisfied, he began to notice the clean yet very worn tables, small equally worn counter, and the six other patrons. The three men sitting on bar stools at the counter wearing well-worn coveralls were exchanging friendly conversation. A thirty-something waitress was also participating, indicating a long term association. She looked around, then asked the couple at a nearby table,

"Hay Martha, do you folks need more coffee or anything?"

"Na, thanks anyway, Winnie, time we get moving," Martha replied, then the sixty-something man chimed in,

"We just need to pick up some things next door at Ned's. Martha needs some material, and I need some hinges to fix that damn old shed door, been saying I was goin to do it for a month or two and thought today was the day."

Winnie picked up the coffee pot from behind the counter, walked to Dean's table topped off his coffee cup, and with a cheerful smile, asked,

"Be anything else I could bring you?" Her smile brightens her face clear to the eyes Dean could not help smiling back, something that had not happened since leaving Maggie U. It felt so good on his face that Winnie was given a five-dollar tip, as he followed Martha and her man out the door to Ned's.

Ned's was a general store straight from a movie, taking place in a small farming town. Shelves were overflowing with new articles, right beside others that may have been there when Dean was born.

"Well, how you folks doing," the mustache asked from behind the counter. As the diminutive man and the couple from the cafe continued talking, Dean wished he had a camera. The vast handlebar mustache seemed to have a mind of its own, and the small head holding seemed it was just there for support.

It turned out to be attached to Ned, and his five-foot-six body. Ned even wore a very tired and stained leather apron with a bow tie above it. The Andy Griffin show could have used this guy as part of the storyline. At first, Dean wasn't sure what he was looking for, except for a flashlight and something to snack on. Ned sized Dean up within moments and began suggesting a wide range of camping related items. Even began helping carry the purchases out to the car.

"Now, this just might be a problem," he exclaimed, seeing the Corvette sitting outside. "We just might have to rethink what it is, you can fit into this here vehicle." Dean took over the packing, and Ned continued to suggest and modify the purchases.

Forty-five minutes later, Dean was reviewing while Ned was listing the items and totaling cost. By the time the bill was settled, the Vette loaded, Dean was unsure what was next. With as much camping stuff, packaged foods, and anything else he could stuff into the tiny storage areas of the car he realized that he needed one more thing, a map.

Between Ned, Winnie, her husband the cook, and enough time to collect, stow, pay, and get directions, Dean thought he had a vague plan of attack. But first, it was time for lunch. With belly full, plenty of guidance, and the history of how Winnie and husband Fred bought the Huntsville cafe, named after their last name Hunt, it was time. And not forgetting Ned's help, and the history of his General Store Dean almost felt he was a native of Kerrville Village.

One more time driver's hypnotic trance took over, with Dean becoming more of a passenger than the driver. It was almost like Nam and twenty-four hours a day, sometimes for close to a week at a time. Another part of his brain broke in and brought him back to the present.

What else did he need? Was he forgetting something? Currently, it was to go somewhere and discover something, something that would guide or give purpose. Hopefully, some insight into who the Hell this person was that was driving a Corvette into the mountains.

Maybe an hour or more later, he saw what looked like an interesting spot he thought might work. Easing the car off the road onto two ruts still pretending to be a road and a grassy area off to the side, it just felt right. Out of sight, quiet, and a place to meditate.

What's first? He puzzled, looking at the piles of stuff in the passenger seat holding even more than the space behind the seats. It had never crossed his mind when buying the Vette that it did not actually have a trunk, also that he might actually need one.

Grabbing a large flashlight from the pile, he climbed out and began exploring the clearing. Off in the direction of the sunset, he could hear water, maybe a stream gurgling somewhere nearby, buzzing of insects, an owl hoot, and rustling in the underbrush. Dean had not been a Boy Scout and or any other type of woodsman, so he was unsure of what he was hearing, but it sure was not the sounds of the inner city.

The ground smelled kinda like a lawn and seemed pretty flat, so he went back and grabbed the sleeping bag and what had been labeled a pup tent. He had almost asked Ned the clerk if it was for puppies, but based on the camping stuff around it, he decided it must be a people tent. After about 20 minutes of grunting, cursing, and pulling, he tossed the poles and other stuff to the side, laid the tent material flat on the ground, added the sleeping bag on top, and fell asleep a few minutes after wiggling into it.

Sometime in the morning daylight, he awoke to the sounds of something. Gently turning his head he saw a deer not far away. It was swaying and munching on the vegetation down in front of her or his hooves. Sunshine was warming the back of his neck. His bladder was calling in an urgent manner as he began wiggling out of his cocoon. The wiggling startled the deer, and with his mouth tasting like dirt, eyes feeling gritty, his butt cheeks hurting, and no idea where in the Hell here was, he just stood looking around. Thankfully flight school had included some basic survival training, not something he paid a lot of attention to at the time but something that could help. Once Vietnam operations started, escape, and evasion school had been scheduled, yet never seemed to happen at "a time that was available for him. Now he was in the woods. Noise all around, lots of stuff in the car with all the time needed to learn about camping.

Two hours later, he stood with pride, observing his efforts. A fire pit, a pile of wood, a tent standing tall, and now it was time to investigate the stream he had heard last night. This might just be what he had heard from some of the guys when they were romancing about hunting. Even when taking their family camping.

Now it was him and the woods. A stream nearby to sit by and maybe that deer stopping by. Above everything was the need for a lot of time to think. The log not far away from his newly erected tent seemed to call for a sit-down.

Hot dogs and beans were on his mind, yet the problem was he forgot to get a lighter or matches, oh shit. It took a while, but he finally remembered the Vette had a cigarette lighter, now all that was needed was something to light on fire. Luckily the car came with just what he needed a car manual. Fifteen minutes later, he had managed to get a fire burning, and a stick trimmed completely with a hotdog attached.

Tired, fed, and warm, he watched the night come over the clearing and sat beside the fire pit, watching the fire die down, leaving red coals glowing in the dark night. It was time to begin taking stock of how he had come to this place, both figuratively and literally.

What happened the other day at Maggie U? Dr. D talked about caring, caring about YoYo, his family and how they had died.... Dean began to shutter, then choke, and the tears erupted. He had not let himself review his bailing-out behavior as he what? Ran! Ran from what, Dr. D? His pain? What? What the Hell was that about?

All these years, he had swallowed fear and disgust and tuned out what the bombs he and the crew dropped, including Napalm and agent orange. What would be the outcome of what they were doing to the people, land, and future of this country? He had forced himself not to think of the aircraft that did not return after missions, nor even the ones that burned on the flight deck. Not only from crash landing but also from personnel errors that allowed a sidewinder missile to go active and fire into a cluster of aircraft. The forward part of the angle deck became a fireball, twelve men died, and six aircraft destroyed. These and many other parts of the last four and a half years were ignored, swallowed, and/or discounted.

Not once did he cry, and now he's in God knows where sitting on a log sobbing like a little kid. What the Fuck was wrong with him? He hadn't lost a family like Dr. D had. He hadn't lost his eyes. He hadn't missed anything...except himself, his beliefs, his values, his country.

She had been so right, and he had been so incredibly wrong. YoYo had stood up without weapons and fought for the rights of all people. He had struggled to destroy a country and its people. Now our leaders are talking about calling an end to the war. No matter what they say, we lost after all the deaths, destruction, and devastation.

Dean looked out of eyes that were not seeing, listening with ears not hearing, and emotions that were crashing. Hours later, when the sun was setting, he began to return to a shattered man, with no place to run. He crawled into his sleeping bag and hid.

Early the next morning, he hunted for a proper location for bowel movements. Once found, he completed the task behind a moss cover log. One perfect for sitting and really glad he had that car manual.

Surveying the area, he discovered what appeared to be a trail. Pretending to think like he knew what he was looking at, he decided it just might be a deer trail needing to be explored. Ten minutes and a lot of brush fighting against him, by pushing against arms, face, and chest, he broke through and located the stream. This is what it's all about, he thought. Perching on a boulder, sun warming his back and the sounds all around attempting to gentle his mind.

Rustling noises over by what might be a trail broke into his trance-like stare into the sparkles of rushing currents and the gentle babbling of the rushing water talking to him. Not twenty-five feet away, a deer pranced to the water's edge and began drinking. Dean froze and watched in delight. The deer, what was it called when just a pup, maybe a buck, no a fawn, he didn't know. The magic of the moment made it a non-issue.

The enormous brown eyes spotted him, it twitched, stared, glanced down, back up, then returned to drinking, Dean had been accepted well… for the moment. He moved his leg to get a better hold, and the deer-friend exploded into action, bounding across the stream and into the brush. Guess accepted wasn't exactly right. Maybe Dean was just part of the scenery which pretty much summed up how he was feeling out here in nowhere land.

Getting to his feet and heading back to camp thinking, which soon turned to confusion, and then just feeling lost. Lost in the woods. In this country. In this connection. Or was it an issue with or about YoYo, plus whatever the Hell Dr. D was talking about.

"Shit" who in the Hell am I, screaming in his head. Who in the bloody Hell am I and what the Hell am I Supposed to do!

He began to walk, head down, just moving forward. He just kept plodding forward until he came to a thicket, a thicket with only a small hollow at the base leading into the depth. Looking around, then around some more, the path leading him here wasn't a path but just a tiny trail through tall grasses. Maybe for small rodents, rabbits, squirrels, and things like that followed, it.

How did he…get here? And where was here? Backtracking became less than helpful, little trails went off here and there. Some looked like he might have used them, others clearly did not. After trying three different ones, worry started seeping in.

Catching his breath and taking some more calming slow breaths in, hold one, two, three, exhaling, again, one, two, three. Sit on a big rock, calm your thoughts, slowly scan around, look for clues, listen.

There, what is that? The stream, I think it is, listen, yes, that's it. Go back down that way, the sounds are to the right, look for a path leading that way. This continued until Dean could hear the sounds of water becoming louder.

Speeding his pace and trying hard to observe the direction. Where the sun was overhead, maybe a little more that way. Would it indicate he was going west? The path begins to widen where others had joined, soon it was more than a rodent trail and was becoming a distinct trail, and sounded like it was leading to the water.

Trees, shrubs and blackberries, a tree that looked chopped down, someone had been here. Thirty or forty feet farther down the path was a massive rock formation dead ahead, the path veering to the right of it. The nearer he came to a turn in the road, the more he was confident it had to be a human-made path. Rounding the massive boulder brought a worn and tired looking shack into view. Dean had to pause for a moment before accepting that it was a shack. The moss covering the roof and the weathered wooden sides seemed more in place with the forest than something man-made.

This was something out of a movie or novel. A few cones of the sun filtered through the trees. Providing a dusky lighting effect around the cabin. Several birds of different species and their songs provided a melody with the sounds of water, the background orchestra. Now all the scene needed was little red riding hood to come skipping into the picture.

Dean was hungry, tired, and confused. Everything that was happening said he was lost, yet without threat. As he approached the cabin, the musky smell of forest and buzz of birds, insects, water rushing across rocks filled the background as his feet crunched pine needles and underbrush. The moss-covered roof and a broken window suggested the cabin had long been ignored; Silence broken by the sound of a Crow's caw. He found himself wondering if that was a warning, a welcoming, or just the sound of a forest.

Stepping up on to the porch gently, testing its safety, he was pleased with how solid it felt. The door was unlocked and did not protest to being opened. Dean began to fantasize of being pulled into a, well a kind of hug by the cabin and the surroundings.

It was kind of creepy and/or maybe just plain silly all at the same time. Then the caw of a crow sounded again, this time close, he looked up, and it was on the corner of the roof and appeared to be looking right at him. A tingle on his neck, caught him way off guard. The feeling of being part of a movie or maybe a novel was so strong it caused him to catch his breath, to settle his nerves.

"Oh, that's crap," he uttered, remembering he was a combat veteran, not just a naive city boy.

"Screw it!" he thought while stepping into the cabin and closing the door behind him, "Why in the Hell did I close that, and started to reopen it, then didn't. A manly shrug of his shoulders, and with that began looking around.

One room, an old small cast iron heater/stove in the center of the back wall. A rough wooden frame built against another wall, including what looked like something that might have been a small mattress long ago. And a hand-built stool with a little matching table kinda in the middle of the room. The shelf on the other wall had an old-time styled kerosene lantern and a tin plate, spoon, and fork.

Then crow "CAW," and Dean damn near dove for cover. Spun around to see if it had somehow come inside, not so, it just sounded like it. Nerves jittering, pulse-pounding he casually bolted for the door as he slammed it behind him, taking a couple of slow deep breaths and decided to explore the area. One thing stood out that was more substantial than the cabin was that boulder. For sure, it was huge and looked like a god-like being just sort of dropped it here. It was just out of place. Lots of boulders and other rock formations were around the stream, but they seemed to belong. This giant demanded to be explored.

What Dean suspected would be a hard climb turned out to be more of a hike than a climb. On one side, a fissure provided something that resembled a path leading to the top. The watchtower view at the top was magnificent, especially out on a promontory projecting thirty or more feet over the stream far below.

Squatting down onto his buttocks, he carefully scooted to the edge to dangle his feet over the edge. The sensation triggered memories of breaking through the clouds when climbing to altitude after take off. Time would seem to stand still and it was as if he was an eagle floating in a gently moving river of air. The difference in this day is when this similar sensations took over, he did not have to stay conscious of the aircraft he was flying. Nor what his job entailed. Time disappeared, stress dissipated, time fell away.

"CAW, CAW" broke the revelry. Dean jerked, felt himself starting to slip, caught himself just as he began to move off the edge, and finally grabbed an edge stopping the slide.

"Fuck! Fuck, shit, What the Fuck!" he shouted, then catching his breath, and scooting back from the edge.

"CAW," above and to the side, another crow was standing not more than four or five feet away, staring at him. Dean stared back and, if asked at that moment, would have sworn the damn crow's next sounds where chuckles.

Waving his arms, shouting, "Get the Hell out of here," at the crow. It hopped a step away, cocked its head, and made the chuckling sounds. Looking around Dean scooped up a handful of pebbles tossed them toward the black ragged looking stupid bird as it flapped wings twice, avoiding the stones and landed a foot closer to Dean.

"CAW" looked him in the eye for a moment and gently fell into flight off its perch. A memory flash from Nam, when A MiG fighter locked on Dean's ass. It was a "Grab your ass you are going to die" moment.

Dean's aircraft was slower, less maneuverable and lacked any weapons. Then for an unknown reason the MiG broke lock-on, pulled along side Dean and made a finger gun gesture, rolled his aircraft and departed.

Shaking, cursing, and now shivering, Dean stood and climbed back down and headed to the cabin. Darkness was closing in, and he was sure the shivering was from a chill in the air and not from that stupid bird.

Approaching the cabin, he began gathering twigs, leaves, and other small pieces of wood. Carried his bundle into the cabin and placed most of it into the stove. Then stood there looking around and trying his best to pretend there was a way to start his bundle on fire.

Less than ten minutes later, standing on his watchtower, he began searching for any signs of life. Finding nothing, he turned to head back down when a bright glint flashed. He knew that type of glint it was the sun reflecting off of glass or something else shiny. Not too far in the distance was his Vette, Holy shit.

Slipping twice on the way down and skinning an elbow plus his left hand, he reached the ground and headed down the path from earlier in the day. Within ten minutes, he came to a triad right, left, or straight ahead. The light was fading fast. In the forest, it was closing more quickly.

Not able to remember coming on these splits in the path earlier, he chose to keep moving forward. By the third step, he heard,

"CAW," behind him. Glancing behind there, the stupid damn thing was. Standing in the path looking straight at him,

"CAW" it said bobbing its head.

"CAW."

"Screw you," Dean mumbled and continued down the path. At the most, he took three, maybe four more steps, and something hit his ball cap with a splatting sound. He looked behind him and saw the crow walking away down the path, it looked back and "CAWed."

Dean cursed, pulled the hat from his head and really began

swearing, the fucking bird had shit on him. Finding a rock, he spun and began to throw, at nothing, the bird wasn't there, "Shit." Then he caught himself chuckling at the connection, then turned and began walking.

"CAW," Splat, "CAW." "That's it!" shouting, turned, still holding the rock and then threw it as hard as he could. With a wing flap and hop, the bird was on a low branch and "CAW."

Dean cursing began running at it. Stumbled, grabbed another rock, threw it and missed. The crow with another wing flap landed on the path and started walking down it, back turned as if to say screw you, or maybe a big ha! Ha!

That was more than Dean could take; he started running, cursing, stumbling, and chasing. Panting, sweating, and cursing Dean stopped to catch a breath with hands on his knees he laughed and then just sat down and continued laughing.

"For God's sake, I'm chasing a damn bird," he panted between laughs, "What's going to happen if I catch the damn thing, demand that it stand up and fight like a man!" He laughed until tears were rolling down his cheeks.

Then again "CAW!" There, the damn thing was again, standing in the middle of one of the other two paths splitting off from this one. It just stood there, waiting, turned took two hops down that path, stopped "CAW," and Dean could swear the damn bird winked at him.

What the Hell! OK, let's take that path he yelled and started walking toward the bird. Each time he got within a few feet, the bird would do the wing flap and hop away farther down the path. Dean followed, thinking this had to be the most idiotic thing he had ever done, but at least the damn thing had quit shitting on him.

Thirty minutes later, he was in the clearing looking at the Corvette. CAW was not in sight, had he really started calling it that? With a loud chuckle and snort, he turned to the issue at hand and knew it was time to get something to eat.

After another night sleeping on the ground, he would return to the cabin. A full moon was rising in the early night lighting the clearing. He had never been a camper, but this sure was incredibly beautiful. Finding his way back to the cabin would be at best a fifty/fifty chance in the dark, so it was time to use the cigarette lighter, car manual, and start a fire.

Sitting next to the morning fire as he was sorting out options and wondering if he could find his way back to the cabin, "CAW" came from up high in a nearby tree. He ignored the sound, knowing it wasn't the same one. A flap of wings and then a big black ragged crow landed on a pile of supplies, tied on the back of the Corvette, "CAW!

Not the same one, can't be, he thought as the ugly damn thing hopped down and hooked a chunk of an uneaten hotdog bun. Then flew back up to the pile of supplies and had breakfast.

Shaking his head, while finishing a morning candy bar, Dean decided to load the knapsack. Feeling thankful, Ned suggested he might need one. After Dean thought for a moment, his advice made sense. From that point on, Dean placed his tenderfoot ways in the hands of Ned. After it was all said and done, he was even more grateful for Ned and his general store. Without a doubt, Dean needed to return and purchase matches and anything else he might need or forgot. But first, he had to tote all these supplies to the cabin.

Today the hike to the cabin was much more comfortable than he had suspected. His journey to the cabin the day before had left many scuff marks in the dirt, helping to lead the way. Well, and the sound of caws that came from the ugly ass crow he had evidently named CAW. Dean still was not willing to believe the damn thing was actually guiding him, but…Well, no buts, it was just a coincidence.

Dean smiled as he thought about those cowboy movies he had watched long ago. It always seemed the hero was able to find his way by things like broken branches and such. Now he was the cowboy, and not doing too bad, back pat, back pat.

Three trips later, all the supplies and even the tent were relocated to the cabin. The good news was he did not have to sleep on the ground. The floor of the cabin would do for today, thank you. He would attempt to fix up the bed frame tomorrow.

Dean had been wise enough to bring a note pad from the car. Sitting on the tired old chair, he began to jot down a list starting with matches, blanket, candles, and… The biggest problem was knowing what else he might need. He guessed that would depend on how long he would be here. After what happened with Dr. D., Dean did not think he was in much of a hurry to return to Maggie U.

Finishing his list, he looked around the inside of the cabin one last time. Jotted down a couple of things, then grabbed the knapsack and went out the door. Took a deep breath of forest air, stepped off the porch, and felt a need for a bowel movement. Saying, "Oh shit!" he began searching for a convenient location. He had not explored much around the sides and back of the cabin as of yet. He began searching around the left side did not find what he was looking for. Then found a spot just behind it, a well-positioned log. Just as he was finishing his business, he looked past the right side of the cabin. It was only maybe fifteen or twenty feet from that side. Almost hidden by vines crawling up the side. He had located something he had never actually seen for-real. It was a for real outhouse. The door was reluctant to open, but he got it open with a hard pull resulting in a loud squeal. Surprisingly he knew one more thing that had been forgotten, toilet paper. The door could be fixed, but toilet paper not so much.

Hiking back to the car, Dean found himself stopping, smelling, and well just looking. This he thought was nirvana. He was unsure where he had heard the word or how he knew it meant something like a perfect place of being. Eden, peace, serenity, well, something like that. He wasn't sure what it really meant, but this moment, in this place, it felt like all that. The one thing he knew is that it was the very first time that he could remember feeling anything like this.

A deep intake of the smells, sights, and maybe three steps,
CAW!

CHAPTER FIVE

Leaving CAW

Peck, peck, Peck, peck, woke Dean from a sound sleep, rolling over as his sleep fogged mind attempted to place the sound.

"No luck, shit might as will roll out of the sack, need to take a look," he complained, putting his bare feet on the cold cabin floor.

"Damn, need to keep my socks on," he mumbled, jerked and spun around to the sound of Peck, peck, Peck, peck. CAW's big Brown eye was staring through the broken window pane. The damn bird was becoming a significant pain in the ass.

Opening the door, Dean looked out and loudly asked,

"What the Hell do you want?" The response was

"CAW!" Dean responded with,

"What? And Caw replied with,

" CAW!" Feeling foolish, Dean slipped on some shoes and still in undershorts, stepped off the porch, took another ten steps, and relieved himself, then with a sigh of relief turned and headed back into the cabin. Time to get dressed and start the day.

As he stepped through the door jam, "CAW!" Dean came close to relieving himself one more time, the damn bird was perched on top of the door. Dean had not closed it when he went out, nor when he returned. Need to change that behavior, he thought. Now the big brown eye was staring at him again. Yelling at the bird to get out, he reached for the door and began to swing it shut, CAW hopped from his perch, wings gently flared once, and he landed on the back of the old wooden chair by the wobbly table. One more hop, and he was on the table, snatched a leftover piece of bread and enjoyed some breakfast.

It was now day four at the cabin, and CAW was becoming a fixture, a sidekick buddy, or whatever. Dean did not understand what CAW was, but he sure wasn't just any bird. From the day he had gotten himself lost to this morning, that damn ragged ass crow was in sight or cawing somewhere nearby.

For a bird, he did seem to have some manners, which was indicated by not crapping in the cabin, or porch, Corvette, and most of all, not on him. At least not since that time on the path when Dean didn't follow CAW's directions. As soon as that thought crossed his mind, Dean burst out laughing. I gotta be getting crazy! Maybe I belong out here with Bambi and friends!

For the rest of the day, Dean continued to make what repairs he could in the cabin. Cleaned everything possible then collected and stacked as much firewood as he could find. Finishing by making a list of things that needed repairing and what he would need to fix them. The second list of required supplies needed for extending his time here. Plus a plan to call Dr. D. Then returning to Kerrville for filling his two lists and making that phone call felt almost like going out on the town.

Finding his way back without radios, radar, or a navigator was quite the adventure. After a few side trips to nowhere and back, took the better part of five hours. Almost losing hope and feeling totally lost, he finally spotted a sign indicating seven miles to Kerrville. Ten minutes later, he was once again in the bustling metropolis. With his mouth watering up at the thought of a hot meal, he pulled up to the Huntsville Cafe. Parked climbed out of the Corvette stood for a moment stretched and then strolled inside to Winnie's greeting of, "How you doing, Dean?" Dean couldn't stop the big grin erupting across his lips. Damn, he thought this must be like the movies and people having a hometown.

A full hour later, belly full to the point of hurt, and enough coffee to keep him awake until tomorrow he was ready to go visit Ned next door. The doorbells were still dinging when Ned called out a loud "Howdy

Neighbor." Fifteen minutes or more later, he had told Ned all about his adventures, including a bird named CAW. While Ned jumped in with a tale about the big bass he had named Buddy. It seemed Buddy grew to know Ned after a good three to four years. He would show up in the same spot every time Ned would go to his favorite fishing hole. He went on to claim, "Buddy had to be narly 10 pounds and would nose the damn bait, no matter what worms, flies or lures. "Never bite he'd just nudge it, like he was doing a shaking hands thing just in fish language." Ned chuckled.

As the storytelling wound down, Dean began filling the little space behind the Corvette's seats. First, with hammers, nails, and such, then small ice chest Ned suggested would be suitable for keeping some perishables. It barely fit on the passenger's side floorboard, which was now serving as the trunk. He planned to fill it with a steak, bacon, eggs, and a jug of milk. Finishing up, he paused and asked for directions to the town's grocery while making his goodbyes to Ned.

Jumped in the Vette and drove down a block, turned right, and found the local Food Exchange. The Grocer, a tall thin man even taller than Dean, was not quite as trusting and friendly as Ned and Winnie, yet he was still reluctantly helpful. Dean filled a cart with his wish list plus some items, not on the list. Placing the perishables in the ice chest, he hoped Ned was right about it, keeping everything safe for two, three hours. He filled most of the passenger seat with cans, boxes, and jars. Complained about the Corvette's lack of trunk, also about himself buying a car without a trunk. Really Dean, I mean Really! Then tossed in some potatoes, bread, coffee, and sugar.

With a sigh of relief at getting everything stowed, he went back inside and asked the Grocer if there was a telephone he could use. He noticed Dean looking at the phone hanging on the wall behind the counter and directed Dean to a payphone down the block. Stifling what he wanted to say, asked for four dollars worth of quarters. He was told, "Gee Sonny just can't spare that amount of quarters," and instead counted out 10 dimes six quarters and the rest in nickels.

Walking toward the phone booth, he decided to turn back around and bring the Corvette up close to the phone. Mr. Grocer obviously did not trust out of towners or maybe just not some young stranger with a good suntan. Dean re-parked the car, sat and recounted his phone money three times. Got out of the car, turned around, and got back in. Started the car drove to the Cafe and ordered a piece of apple pie with a scoop of vanilla ice cream. Two cups of coffee and forty minutes later he drove back to the phone booth.

The first time he dialed Dr. D's number, it was busy, so he walked around the block then tried again. This time he answered, and before Dean could say more than a couple of words, Dr. D asked for Dean's phone number so he could call him back. He read the number to Dr. D, and before he could say yes or no, the phone went dead. Minutes ticked by, then an hour and then an hour and a half. He started the car cursing quietly under his breath and popped the shifter into reverse. Just as he began to let out the clutch, the phone began to ring.

"Well, son, I did not think you were going to answer for a minute or two. I am grateful you did. Where are you located? I have a lot to discuss with you. How soon may we meet? I can meet you in Bart's Pub later this evening." There was a long pause before Dean was able to clear his mind for a response.

"Are you still there, Dean," Dr. D inquired, which unfroze Dean's mouth but not his mind, "Ah, yeah, and I'm not there, a, I'm here. In a.." For a moment, he could not remember the name of the town, then said:

"I'm in Kerrville Village."

"And where pray tell might that be?" Dr. D responded.

"I have no idea."

"What?" Dr. D asked.

"I drove here after I left your office and really have no idea where, besides in the mountains, if I had to guess somewhere north. What's so important." Silence followed for a few minutes, which was exactly enough time for his anxiety to invade his stomach and mind.

The silence was broken as Dr. D began explaining everything that had transpired since Dean had left. How he and somebody named Dr. Zoie Philmore were planning on transferring Yolanda from the hospital to a place called Aisling House.

"Zoie and I are working towards identifying and developing a support team to assist Yolanda in her recovery. The Aisling is the beginning, now we need to staff it. I have a multitude of ideas, with Zoie, as my cohort in this, I have complete faith Yolanda will begin a successful regime toward recovery. Dean, Yolanda is real fragile in a vast range of issues. The blindness and mental health issues are our primary concern, well currently, that is. We just rescued her from a hospital staff wanting to commit her to a psychiatric inpatient hospital. They also suggested recommending the possibility of electroshock therapy. Along with cold-induced hibernation, drugs such as Thorazine. One of these imbeciles actually spoke of a frontal lobotomy. I sincerely believe that the doctor's suggestion was coming from frustration. Trust me, that just would not be allowed this day and age. If memory serves me right, the last one was performed in 1967."

"Good God! Dr. D! I will leave right now, and, and"

"At this moment in time, we must move forward with the utmost caution. Dean, this is akin to the center of a typhoon, trying to find a place of safety. We need to develop a therapeutic environment in addition to a myriad of supporting components. If you show up too soon, it might just push the envelope to an overwhelming array of emotional and sensory stimulation. At this time, she seems to be struggling just staying cognizant. Dealing with you and the past might just be too much for her."

"But Sir, you said when we last spoke that I could help, you needed my help!"

"True, true, and I still stand by that, just not at this moment. We need to find a way for her mental state to stabilize. She is not only dealing with sightlessness, but she is also dealing with what happened at that demonstration, in addition to months in a comma. These are just the primary issues. There are also a plethora of seemly lesser complications surrounding what we have already identified.

Please hear when I say the first and most important priority is establishing a tranquil environment for her to begin rehabilitating. We are very, very close. In a month or maybe more, I hesitate to estimate at this time. I implore you to call every week to receive updates on our outlook and her progress. I urge you to support us as we assemble all the necessary components needed for her recovery.

I am fully cognizant of what will assist her recovery. It is my firm belief your presence in the near term will be very beneficial. She will need your support. It is also my belief that she still cares deeply, also Zoie and I will be thankful for all your love for her. Currently, it is imperative I meet with Professor Hanson. I believe we will be providing an encouraging update next week. It is my hope to hear from you at this day and time each week, Son."

As Dean began forming a response, the line went dead, and the dial tone buzzed in his ear. He tried calling back twice to no avail. After that, he dropped the buzzing phone in its cradle, walked to the Corvette, and basically fell into the seat.

Sitting frozen to the seat, mind screaming but making no sense, he heard, "CAW." Then with fluttering and flapping, an ugly ass crow landed on the top back of the passenger seat. One big brown eye staring at him. The townspeople are still talking about the too tall young stranger driving out of town in the bright yellow too small car with no trunk and a big black crow perched on the top of the passenger's seat riding shotgun.

PART FOUR

CHAPTER ONE

ZOIE

When they sat down for dinner, Zoie was interested in what Damon's concerns were. Still, she cautioned the necessity of examining Yolanda before saying anything about getting her released from the hospital. The most significant barrier, outside of getting her released, would be locating a facility appropriate for her.

The two agreed that medical and psychiatric hospitals were not options. Especially with the diagnosis the current physicians were developing. Zoie raised another possible issue about what, if any legal involvement Yolanda could possible be facing. Until Zoie brought it up, Damon had not thought to investigate that potential dark hole.

"I am so entangled in identifying how to disengage her from that hospital," Damon responded. Then he added, "I have been blind to the peripheral issues surrounding her circumstances. Thank you, I truly am incredibly thankful for you, and your heartfelt caring."

"Why thank you, kind Sir, I agree our number one priority is Yolanda's well-being. We will start liberating her first thing in the morning. But for now, may I suggest you and I focus on the two of us."

By the time they finished dinner and returned to Damon's apartment, they were both intellectually exhausted. Yet, physically they found an evening of sexual adventure refreshing for them both intellectually and even more so emotionally.

During a small breakfast, they identified tasks for both of them. Zoie had the job of setting up an appointment with the hospital's Chief Resident and presenting herself as a Psychologist specializing in the newly identified treatment for Post Traumatic Stress Disorder (PTSD). In addition to provide a wide range of information relating to additional trauma issues. With the recently released edition of the Diagnostic and Statistical Manual of Mental Disorders (DSM-III) and a marker for the diagnosis of/and treatment for PTSD as a potent weapon for validating Doctor Zoie Philmore PhD for Yolanda Swiftriver.

Both he and Zoie believed Yolanda was exhibiting DSM III identified erratic behaviors due to the National Guard's attack. In Yolanda's case, the attack was also responsible for her coma and the horrible experience of waking from her coma in a state of blindness.

The current insensitive team of physicians would exacerbate Yolanda's symptoms. This in turn was compounded by the hospital's current medical expert's unfamiliarity with the cluster of PTSD symptoms that Yolanda was exhibiting. This included her inability to intellectually and much of the time emotionally process fear, anger, and other related issues such as trauma. Because in a hospital no one talks to you as a human being-just a bed number.

Zoie continued the conversation by identifying how these issues may have triggered an actively developed psychologically induced defense mechanism of blindness. Then she continued,

"If so, it is also likely the prolonged length of the coma, brain trauma, and chaos of multiple medical staff prodding, poking, and diagnosing had a significant compounding effect on all these issues. Such as significant confusion by differing diagnoses from a multitude of medical experts, thus increasing the development of an already existing defense mechanisms."

Monday morning, Dr. Zoie Philmore prepared to follow through with her part by entering the hospital and arranging a conference with Yolanda's primary physician, Dr. Jamseson. The doctor agreed to meet and presented Zoie with a rigid, let us say, something other than a pleasant personality within a brief amount of time. It could even be referred to as a rigid "A-Hole personality syndrome."

The doctor openly questioned her right to examine his patient and possibly find fault with his, and/or his team's treatment recommendations. Zoie spent most of her energy and time attempting to work through Dr. Jamseson's roadblocks. Her primary difficulty was not portraying any indication of suggesting incompetence within his or the hospital's staff. From the beginning, she cautioned herself to tread lightly by not stepping on toes, especially Jameson's and any of his minions. After all she was questioning their assumptions and suggesting they may not have a solid foundation for their diagnoses.

Zoie had also successfully scheduled a meeting with Dr. Jamseson and his medical Director Dr. Richard Bollinger. It was to take place after the initial meeting with Dr. Jamseson and would also include Dr. Soule, the Dean of the Magnolia's Universities Psychology Department.

Early in the meeting, she began to believe there was a slight decrease in the icy shield she had been battling with Dr. Jamseson. Yet his behaviors continued in a manner indicating superiority. He also began to sermonize at Zoie regarding what she could and could not expect to do. Three minutes into the criticism, he began citing reasons Zoie should not receive permission to examine the patient. He paused, adjusted his glasses, tilted his head back, and directed his nose at Zoie and stated,

"Permission for this," paused for a few seconds then continued, "this , individual, in my professional opinion, should not be granted for the patient's sake." As the statement left his mouth, Jamseson looked towards the Director as if expecting agreement.

Zoie fought to practice all manners of emotional self-control before responding. Before the Director had a chance to speak. She began her response to Jamseson's diatribe starting by dissecting the hospital's arguments. This began with the importance of including a consulting psychologist with a background in PTSD and a new set of eyes. She continued by describing how this would exemplify the hospital's desire to explore all treatment options. Next, she gave a detailed review of Zoie and Damon's earlier analysis of Yolanda's treatment regiment. Emphasizing in vivid detail, the lack of the patient's recent progress and Yolanda's "on the record" stated issues with the treatment team's current treatment recommendations.

Then with heart in hand, Zoie said, "I believe the majority of individuals inside the Marigold Hospital and the thousands like them are dedicated helpers. The problem is they were trained to help much in the same way a mechanic is trained. Repair and or replace parts on the car, plane, or train they are working" on.

I am in no way attempting to demean the incredibly hard-working and highly educated individuals inside these walls. My expertise is analyzing the difference between repairing the individual and healing the individual. Yolanda has been "repaired" from the coma. She has not had an opportunity to heal emotionally and possibly even from her chronic physical injuries. The patient needs a safe, quiet, and nurturing environment, if there is any hope, for this healing process. I believe myself and Dr. Damon Soule have the ability to provide that environment when we are afforded that opportunity. With all respect you, Doctor Richard Bollinger are the only one that can offer us that opportunity.

The Director's facial expression and his vocal tone reflected respect when he acknowledged the patient herself was voicing issues related to his hospital and the treatment team. He did not reveal that he had earlier initiated a plan for identifying undocumented and in-house knowledge of the patient's concerns. These documented issues alone encouraged him to consider Dr. Zoie Philmore's request. That and what he had unofficially uncovered from the nursing staff. The combination ensured his inability to disprove additional expertise. Rejecting what was being offered would be seen as a detriment to the patient and, more importantly, the hospital.

The patient's chart contained the Charge Nurse's notes indicating the patient during the last four days had been requesting a discharge. Now that information was openly outside of Director Bollinger's ability to repress. The patient was on record of also overhearing Dr. Jamseson's conversations. That included three individuals of his treatment team, saying:

"If we discharge this problem to the Hillside Psychiatric Hospital, we will be done with it."

The nursing staff also heard these comments, which was indeed a nail in the proverbial coffin. Yolanda's chart also indicated the patient had been making significant progress for almost three weeks before these complaints, that was nail number two.

The notes also indicated a lack of progress, coinciding with the same time frame. The patient also began complaining about her treatment and requesting discharge. The two professionals, Zoie Philmore, PhD. and Damion Soule, PhD. standing before him presented detailed documentation of this information, in addition to the reasons for the demands and the patient's right to make them. The genuine deciding factor was they also could make all these issues public. Based on all these factors, Director Richard Bollinger's favorite baseball umpire would say with robust enthusiasm,

"You're out of here!" in regard to this patient's discharge.

CHAPTER TWO

Hanson Folks & Aisling House

Leaving the Director's office, Damon and Zoie attempted to restrain from shouting with joy and breaking out in a dance. Zoie was the moderator and, in a low voice, continued to calm Damon's jubilation until they got into his car. He gave a gallant try, that lasted two, maybe three steps after stepping out the hospital's exit, before grabbing Zoie in a hug and twirling around in a circle. Her kiss prevented his scream of joy being heard outside of her mouth.

On the drive to Damon's apartment, Zoie continued to explore Yolanda's current behaviors, starting by saying:

"I need your ear to bounce off my thoughts. I believe Yolanda obviously suffered a loss of consciousness, then post-traumatic amnesia, disorientation, and confusion. All of which began immediately following the tear gas grenade induced traumatic brain injury.

Above all, these symptoms suggest a need for a healing environment that will be diametrically opposite of her current situation. The first thing that I know would benefit her is a significant decrease in all stimuli. Yolanda needs a treatment team focused on healing the human, not just biology." She explained to Damon emphasizing these were her responsibilities. Then she concluded with,

"I believe I have an answer to many, but not all of Yolanda's and our needs. The first thing I need to accomplish is finding an environment to provide this before I would be willing to considering removing her from that damn hospital. So I need my Hero Damon to rescue the fair maiden Yolanda, and myself, of course."

"This hero needs to discuss several occasions when I was sitting by her bed. At first, she moved in and out of consciousness and spoke and behaved as if she saw and talked to people who told, or a better word would be taught her things. I am not sure how to word this except Yolanda believed she was one of them, perhaps part of a tribe. My first impression was she was describing dreams, then maybe hallucinations. Still these experiences seemed, at times, to continue even after she regained consciousness," He paused for a moment unsure what to say.

Zoie took his pause as an opportunity to review with him Yolanda's traumatic experience. How it was not abnormal for individuals to experience dream-like visions, especially one such as Yolanda's.

"Damon, Yolanda is terrified, and her visions are a cry for help, a cry for safety, and above all, more than anything a plea for understanding. She has not received any of what I just said, except for myself and you. If we, no, when we secure a place of safety for her, I have no doubt the visions will begin to dissipate. Thank the stars none of what you just disclosed was indicated in her chart. Not from nursing or doctors, and I assume you have not discussed this with anyone."

"Good God no, I considered what she was saying came from the drug cocktails they were giving her. Her descriptions sounded a lot like what Hippies describe from those hallucinogenic drugs they take. Yolanda dropped out of school and became part of that movement, culture, and I don't know the group. She even talked to me about professors doing that junk. I must admit I thought about that in addition to what the hospital prescribed."

"Now the good news, I believe I have a plan to resolve what we have been discussing." Three hours and five different phone call later, he located Professor Hanson Folks and discovered he was also planning on contacting Damon when the Professor said,

"Coincidently I have thought it is an excellent time to extend you a dinner invitation, would three days from now be acceptable?"

"Perfect," Damon responded," I am also interested in discussing a few topics with you. Would seven o'clock be appropriate?"

After ending the call, Damon reassured Zoie he might have an answer to a wide range of the topics that they had explored.

For the following three days, Damon reviewed how and what he would say to Hanson. Telling himself, Hanson would see the advantage of having Yolanda transferred to Aisling House. After all, Hanson was more than just a mentor to Damon, even more than just a friend. Their relationship had developed into something far more. Hanson was more like a favorite Uncle, or maybe even a Grandfather.

Years ago, this change evolved. But it was only two Thanksgivings ago when Professor Hanson Folks sat him down by the fireplace at Aisling House, looked Damon in the eye and requested Damon start referring to him by his nickname Hans. For a few months, Damon attempted to use Sir instead, but Hanson would reprimand him and insist his name was Hans.

Later that evening, Damon assured Zoie a plan he had devised for moving Yolanda to a perfect environment would succeed. Then he began describing the relationship he and Chancellor Folks developed over the years, saying,

"My close relationship with Hans and what I like to think of as the charismatic power of Zoie added to my incredible power of reason will be all we need." They both chuckled over the statement and continued to plan. Both feeling confident in their ability to enlist Hans' blessing, or on second thought, more accurately his assistance. He was the key they needed, and more important, Yolanda needed it.

Reaching across the table to take Zoie's hands, he continued,

"When he does agree, the next primary issue is identifying 24-hour assistance by a caretaker."

" Yolanda needs to work with a caregiver, not be taken care of by a caretaker, Damon. She is just beginning to explore the concept of becoming empowered instead of being an invalid. She needs to get away from the damned hospital! Almost everybody treats her as either a piece of meat to be turned, prodded, or seasoned!" Zoie forcibly stated, with her gray eyes darkening. Then after pushing his hands away Zoie continued,

"She needs someone like Helen Keller had with Anne Sullivan. A relationship built on mutual respect. This is assuredly the only possible avenue for her to flourish instead of living in defeat. And you and everyone else better get on board this train if she has a chance. Do you want her to be the person that impressed you? One that you are proud of, and even learned from or someone cowing in the corner of darkness?"

The ferocity in Zoie's voice and eyes resulted in a loud scraping sound as Damon pushed his chair back, with a shiver trickling down his neck,

"I get it! Really! I'm with you. It's the whole purpose of getting her out of there and I hope into Aisling House," he said, reaching to re-take her hand. As soon as their palms connected fingers interlaced, her eyes lost the flaming glare, and she paused looked down and said, "Wow, sorry. That took me totally by surprise. I must say I knew I cared about Yolanda, but I guess I really did not know it was anywhere near this level. I know you know and understand, and well, I just know. Maybe I need you to help me hold on to my professional side a little more tightly than this Mother Avenger side. At least long enough to accomplish our goals."

Three days later, he was driving along the tree-lined road leading to the Manor, wondering about what was going to transpire, off and on he slowed the car to a crawl, rehearsing the most effective way to encourage Hans to allow Yolanda's transfer to the Manor. Even as he was doing this, Zoie's earlier behaviors finagled their way into his thoughts.

As he was breaking to a stop in front of the Aisling, he shouted: "Good Goddamn, I'm totally falling in love with her." That realization drowned all the rehearsing which had earlier consumed him.

Several deep, deep breaths helped him to quiet his thoughts of Zoie long enough to get his mind back on track. His stomach, neck, and intellect were all playing havoc with his ability to reassert a calm, clear, rational scientific brain. Instead, he was edging toward fermenting anxiety as he remembered his last words with Yolanda. He began replaying his ignorant behavior before leaving the hospital. Yolanda now believed he was going to help. He had to make this work! Not a choice!

Yesterday his excitement was off the charts with so many answers, and possibly finding more, now found his thoughts escaping from his brain into words,

"We have a place, a safe place and will soon move you…" trailing off as he heard what his mouth was saying.

"Ah, Ah, what I mean… Is there a possibility that…, Well damn, I think Zoie and I have come up with a possible plan. If it works, this will allow us to take you to Aisling House. That is until you can get back on your feet, is what I mean."

"That's incredible, Dr. D, really! I'm getting out of this! Now that is great news. Where, when, soon, I hope. Tell me everything." Yolanda's excitement bubbled forth.

All this and more was crowding his mind and fighting for space. As he struggled to quiet the chaos overtaking his mind. With his head down, he walked slowly on the path leading to the massive front doors. The insecurity battling to the extent that he actually started to turn around and leave, for just a moment. Instead, with palms sweating and anxiety seemingly floating in the air before him he turned back toward the door, reached for the door clapper,

"Clang, Clang," broke his mind's chaos allowing him to ignore how devastating it would be if he were unable to recruit Hans into the plan.

With swirling questions and thoughts fighting to invade, he waited for the doors to open. As minutes passed, the concerns became louder. How would Yolanda's emotional and psychiatric issues interface with returning to a place like this? How would she navigate a situation of this size? The questions just continued without answers.

What effect would Dean have on her? What about the regression studies, are they possible? Would Dean even be willing to reengage in the research? The first hurdle would be gaining permission to set up a research lab at the Manor. There were additional issues surrounding Dean's dropping out of sight for over two weeks, and will he even be willing to see her. Possibly his biggest hurdle might be what he had disclosed to Dean. These, along with a myriad of other questions, need to be considered.

Demanding his mind to become quiet, he took a deep breath and shouted,

"Shut up," and the door silently began to swing open, Oh God, I hope that shout was just inside! And Hans said, "So, tell me all about Yolanda."

CHAPTER THREE

How the tapestry began

An Owl hooted, Dances-as-Rain looked behind her into the dark, yellow eyes staring back at her. Looking back around, she was looking into the bonfire flames and a gathering of women. Through the fire and smoke all the elders were sitting in the west. Face painting, robes, and implements of power identified the Walk-a-La woman as, She-elder Womb-Wise, that Dances labeled the Medicine Woman. Now knowing her as the teacher of "Mysteries, The Skills, and The Way." All these titles belonged to her, who was the caller to this fire.

Crackling and snapping, sparks raising toward the moon, lighting a cone, reaching toward the sky. Flames were rising and dancing on a pyramid of newly stacked cedar called to the clan's omen. A soft drum beat sounded in rhythm with the licking flames providing a rhythm for their dance to the sky. She-elder spoke of creation, acceptance, and most of all the Mysteries. The hypnotic beat of the drums were weaving with her musical voice rhythms. Dances-as-Rain saw She-elder's words flowing from her mouth and floating cloud-like toward her until the words surrounded Dances. All else faded, and the words became a vision.

"Untold thousands and thousands of moons ago,
Mother Earth, the ground we stand in,
was formed under the endless sky above."

And the rhythmic moaning of the pubescent girls sitting in the east highlighted the vision with clouds and the smell of new rain.

"Father Sun and Sister Moon" watched,
the tapestry of past, present, and future,

weave the plains, mountains, rivers, and seas."

And the humming of the childbearing women on the south made the burbling streams and whispering winds.

"The Great Spirit not finished,

wove trees, herbs, corn,

and all the plants covering the land."

And the chanting of the girls to be wedded made the plants growing all across the land.

"The Great Spirit continued,

weaving all the animals,

wolves, bears, coyote, and all the rest."

And sounds of coyote and wolf erupted, from the throats of the warrior woman's, to paint the animals that traveled the land.

"Than all that flew in the sky above,

eagle, hawk, crow,

owl, robins, and butterflies."

And the young and old sang the sounds of crow, hawk, and eagle, while the youngest fluttered as the butterflies.

"Still the weave continued,

all that lived in the ground,

moles, worms, ants."

And the woman of age sitting in the north murmured for all that lived within the ground.

"Last the Great Spirit,

wove all that walked,

on two feet,

the people."

And they all drummed their feet to show the people walking the ground.

"All this and more,

Did the Great Spirit,

WEAVE."

And all sang, chanted and danced in honor of the weave.

As the sounds died away, once more her voice rose and reached out and sang,

"When Dances-as-Rain was woven,

Owl was sent to catch you as you fell.

Now you become a student of the Mysteries."

Yolanda sat bolt upright in her bed and began to shutter, shiver, and then started questioning. What just happened, what does it mean, and who am I?

CHAPTER FOUR

The Plan With Hans

Zoie had left his apartment, giving him a passionate kiss, hug, and then ran out the door to complete the next part of her mission. Leaving Damon's mind in a whirl thinking, Where did that fit? We went from friends… to closer friends… to lovers?

If nothing else, he knew she loved helping, especially those who she bonded with. Yolanda and Zoie from the very beginning had more than just a therapeutic patient relationship. Zoie was now an integral member of the team, but had they also became a couple? These thoughts brought him a deep emotional heart boost giving a joy he hadn't experienced, at least not after his wife died.

"This may be a time for healing, not just for Yolanda, but for myself," was a thought from a place he had not considered. It had been inconceivable until this moment. How he felt about Zoie and Yolanda were floating all around his in his heart and mind. On top of these feelings, or was it under them, what he needed to accomplish was attempting to receive professional attention. Instead, his next revelation was this was also the first time in a long time, that his research was beginning to trigger real research type excitement.

All of this was flowing in and out of his mind and emotions. Amongst all of it, Dean had returned, and Damon had to accept responsibility for embedding him into the maelstrom. And how does he fit, or does he? His thoughts were racing like the rapids of water cascading down a flooding stream that's turning into a raging river. His emotions were akin to the canoe without a paddle bouncing around amidst the rapids.

The loss of Dean had set his research back significantly, he guessed in the neighborhood of a couple of years or more. Yolanda, on the other hand, had continued to participate. Yet, it was crystal clear her head just was not in a place for her to be entirely focused. Without intensity, her regression experiences resembled memorized recitals from past experiences instead of in the moment reports.

Then came her involvement with all the furor related to civil and human rights. Watching the assassination of a president, his brother, and later of a man whom Yolanda believed to be one of the greatest in generations, Dr. Martin Luther King. All this was pushed to the background by a lobed tear gas canister, hitting her in the head. Now she is blind. And I expect her to continue helping me? Really, am I actually that shallow and crass? He thought with disgust.

This girl needs my help! I do not have an answer on how that's going to happen. The phone rang, breaking into his thoughts. He walked away from the window, picked up the receiver, and in the next few moments, his dilemma had a possible solution. This was beginning to sound like the breakthrough he needed. Now all the floating and flowing pieces felt like they seemed to be coalescing a bit more. A little like a jigsaw puzzle pieces fitting into place at the right time.

The key to the puzzle was when Hans decided it was a perfect opportunity for a vacation with his family. He had been itching for years to follow through with his promise to the family that when he retired they would have an extensive vacation. Now was that time and he believed the family would agree it was time to set sail. The University winter break would be ending in two weeks, and Hans had told Damon he had been planning to explore the possibility of Damon residing at the Aisling while they were at sea. Damon accepted with joy, even forgetting why he had been attempting to contact Hans in the first place.

Now with any, luck, he would not only have a reason to spend time at the estate but also have a perfect place to move Yolanda. He would also have ample opportunity to resume his research. A gift that could fulfill his desire for finding ways to bring his experiments to fruition without the Department's awareness, mostly without Swintnt's. Otherwise there was potential for conflict, well considerable conflict from Swintnt and the rest of the Department, and probably the university itself. It is what had stopped him until now. He needed a secure and safe place from prying eyes.

With a secure location, he now would have a legitimate facility to move Yolanda for her continuing rehabilitation. She would also be situated in a perfect setting for participating in the research project. If and when that could become beneficial for both of them. The Aisling would provide Yolanda a place of security and serenity outside of the chaos, chemicals, and anxiety around her every day in her present location. No more nurses would be checking and sampling. Doctors would not be diagnosing and suggesting psychiatric hospitals and involuntary commitment. Her home base would be secure without constant hospital-type interruptions

Earlier in their research and before she was injured, she was the first to suggest looking into John C. Lilly's experiments utilizing sensory deprivation. Initially, Damon was resistant to her suggestion and, to be honest, afraid it would lead to involving illicit drugs like LSD. Instead, Yolanda was thinking only about the power of sensory deprivation concerning their experimental studies. She believed in the sensory deprivation tank as a means of increasing her focus.

The tank would allow her and other research subjects to float in a lightless, soundproof tank filled with a mixture of water and Epsom salt, mimicking weightlessness. With water close to skin temperature, individuals were very close to an inside the womb experience. Controlling all of these perimeters would, in effect, decrease the sensory input of the person to almost nil. Damon was initially opposed to the idea because John C. Lilly himself encountered considerable controversy around the use of LSD outside of the tank and also in the tank. To be truthful, the hesitation of experimenting with the tank was also about the possibility of Swintnt breathing down his neck and attempting to discredit Damon's research.

The more he thought about what the tank could do, the more he convinced himself it would help Yolanda. He just had to find out if her thoughts had changed because of all of her recent experiences. He had a real opportunity to provide a way to experience total tranquility, an environmental escape.

With her incredible susceptibility to hypnotic regression, he was unsure whether she was the appropriate person to pursue this therapeutic approach. Damon came to the conclusion it was time to follow Zoie's lead in how to approach Yolanda. A primary reason for recruiting Zoie's participation as a cohort was ethical considerations. She would be responsible for developing Yolanda's psychotherapy. His hope was to engage her in what he was thinking. Hopefully, she would see the value of regressing Yolanda to the time of her injury before and during the campus demonstrations.

Damon was becoming more and more convinced this avenue had a strong possibility of breaking Yolanda's possible psychosomatic blindness. Now was the ideal time needed to develop a research model, acquire the tank, and encourage both Zoie and Yolanda to explore these ideas. Hoping all this was as valid outside his head and in the open as it seemed inside his head.

Fear was beginning to seep into his thoughts in a myriad of areas. Specifically, instead of the tank helping, it might feed into the terror and pain that has been surrounding her. The heartache from the collapse of her and Dean's relationship, the demonstration, attacks, coming out of the coma, then being blind.

"What the hell was he thinking? He might be the one to push her into the abyss of insanity. Once again, is it me… or is it her that I'm trying to help? Sometimes I'm not so sure it's not me that needs to go to a psychiatric hospital. Besides, where would he find the resources for enough financial support to acquire and make operational one of these isolation tanks. The university funding such a project was clearly out of the question."

Before the National Guard attack, Yolanda had begun verbalizing increased interest in continuing her studies and participating in his regression research. Then she just up and disappeared, until the hospital called. Zoie might be the key to the whole puzzle. A puzzle he had become so immersed in that his ability to be objective was failing. He needed to keep himself an objective scientist, or he would surely be contaminating the study and possibly pushing Yolanda over the cliff to a real psychotic break.

Zoie could keep him from committing the biggest sin he could imagine, and that was to let his ambitions hurt a person he secretly loved like a daughter. He hoped he wasn't diving into a pool of transference, yet knew he was. If nothing else proved this, it was his awareness that thoughts like these were increasing. Might this be a way he was subconsciously attempting to compensate for the loss of his daughter instead of preforming valid research?

"Stop IT!" he shouted inside his head as the pain of losing his family hit…

"This just wasn't about that. I care, but it's not the same," He said out loud, and knew he needed to call Zoe and, and…what?

That evening Damon finished packing his evening pipe, ruminating on where to start the conversation. He looked up as Zoie inquired, "What was it you mentioned on the phone earlier today about wanting to discuss something else this evening? Was it something about moving Yolanda to this mysterious Aisling place?"

"Not specifically. Well, it was more about you and I at Aisling House, and Yolanda too," before he finished Zoie inquired, "It would be very beneficial if you could tell me more about this home of Professor Folks."

CHAPTER FIVE

Aisling House and Father Folks (Foireis)

Damon remembered seeing a young woman sitting on a bench, staring out at the ships. How it instantly brought back memories of the stories. Stories of how Aisling House was conceived and built for the love of Hans's Great Grandfather Sinead's wife. Here he was sitting on the veranda somewhere around a hundred years later, experiencing what Hans described as a similar tale of his father Fredrick's, love for his wife, Olivia.

How his emotions seemed to rotate from happiness to sadness when he had been watching Hans's face which seemed to glow when describing his mother. Mainly how her undying love for his father and their family united the family. The same glow dimmed as he began explaining the macabre difference in his father since Olivia passed. Then with glassy eyes disclosing how his father became lost in the hundreds of volumes related to mysticism in the library. He had supported her in every possible way, including the funding of her desire for her passionate search for additions to fuel her knowledge related to the supernatural.

Hans became more animated, telling how his father loved telling the story of how they met. Hans had very little doubt until his father's last day on this earth, anyone that knew him also knew his mother even if they had never met her. Hans said the worst part was how his father, more emotionally than physically, began to deteriorate after her death. At first, he mostly sat in the Aisling at night, staring at pictures of her and their history. Each morning he would dress and arrive at the office no later than seven, he would bury himself in running the business until five or six in the evening, then stop at the club for a drink. As time passed, he would instead just return to Aisling, fix one drink after another drink, think about her, and drink some more.

It seemed when he wasn't mourning her; he searched their library to connect with her spirit. Until she passed, father had been resistant to very few things the two did not agree on except in this case. Still he could not find it in his heart to deny her. The supernatural or what some called the spiritual realm was a concept he never found a way to fit into his logic-based intellect. Father believed the supernatural was just a bunch of foolishness, hocus-pocus nonsense. Yet because of his love for her, he funded money to include and support the massive library here at Aisling House. It was a gift of love from him to her that he was willing to stock the library with an extensive selection of information on what she thought of as the spiritual realm. She knew he was not a believer yet never criticized her as she filled the library with the most modern to the oldest, from the respected to the rejected, with no objections to the expenses.

Frederick's wife Olivia and Barbara Camoran, wife of Hans, became more like Mother and daughter than mother-in-law and daughter-in-law. When the two of them became aware of Hans's star student, that would have course been me, they teamed up in an attempt to pressure Hans into encouraging more research on the spiritual side. They believed hypnosis and regression fit these criteria and could be the stimulus to decrease some of the few quarrels between his Mother and Father. Fredrick typically gave in allowing some concessions, and the most significant was the inclusion of hypnosis plus pre-birth memory experiments.

Hans never revealed this to me. Nor did he explain a lot of other things to me before his Mother's death. One of the most important was that both of the women had included Dr. Byron Swintnt in their campaign for more research in the spiritual realm. Even towards the end, when the treatment for her breast cancer was ineffective, and she was unable to slow the progression, Olivia never gave up her quest, even requesting that Professor Swintnt be allowed to visit.

My impression is Hans's mother always spoke as if mysticism was scientifically factual in all its forms. His father, on the other hand, struggled to balance a desire to support Olivia and maintain his belief in hard science. This struggle began crumbling when hard science was unable to provide an answer to preventing cancer's progression. By the time she took her last breath, and dying in his Father's arms, he had already begun studying texts located in their library. If she suggested one, he would research it intently, and then she would become the teacher and him the student.

One bright spot in all these clouds was when Olivia mentioned Arthur's daughter's wedding to me, one she considered an honest love story. When she and Fredrick talked about their past life experiences, she frequently focused on our love story. Usually bringing some tears of joy as Olivia compared the similarities to her and Fredrick's love story.

I must admit the story of meeting my of wife EmmaRay in a myriad of ways paralleled their story. How we had indeed fallen in love and only six months later, we were engaged, seemingly following a similar path throughout the Folk's family love story history. A story of love at first sight, one that seemed we met our soulmates. And by the way, all this began in the Aisling House's back patio, garden and pool area.

One other genuine exception in this complex story was Hans's brother Robert. Other than Olivia, Robert seemed to be the only other shoulder to lean on. Not only when his brothers were openly critical, but also when his father attempted to encourage him to participate in outdoor activities. Robert's preferences tended to gravitate to the library or spending time with Olivia. Out of all the boys, Robert was the most sensitive and tended to be labeled as a mama's boy. And he showed visible discomfort when the boys attempted to engage him in roughhousing and or sports. Yet when the family members were celebrating or participating in entertaining guests and other social activities, the three boys appeared strongly bonded.

What finally broke the small fragment of heart Fredrick had left happened two years after Olivia's death. The picture perfect marriage that had been a bright spot he and Olivia shared was then shattered. He said, "What came close to break not only my heart but also my spirit was when my wife and two children went shopping and never returned."

EmmaRay was the youngest of daughter Hans' brother Arthur's children and, in a lot of ways, the most serious understudy of Olivia's mystic beliefs. The two were inseparable. My wife in many ways was raised more by Olivia then by her mother JudyAnn

From the day of the accident that killed EmmaRay and our children, Fredrick never gave up his search for any path suggesting a means to connect with her, his own beloved. He believed, and this has to sound, well bizarre, the death of EmmaRay would somehow open a path to his Olivia. He became so consumed in this quest that he stepped down from running his shipping empire and appointed his second-born son Arthur as the head of Folks Shipping. This appointment also resulted in Arthur becoming the sole owner of the company on the day of Fredrick's death. Prior to this, Arthur had made very significant discoveries in his chosen field of biochemistry, innovations that contributed to the studies in DNA research at the time. He was considered one of the brightest newcomers in this field of study.

Initially, he fought his father's desires until he and his wife JudyAnn explored the opportunities this would provide for their family and future. Arthur would have the resources he and his family had dreamed of, instead of just getting by on a scientist's income. It opened up a world of new challenges to feed his mind and allow his wife and children to follow their dreams. The only hesitation for Arthur after accepting these acknowledged benefits was what would happen to his Father. Would stepping down from running the company hurt his father's ability to function or help?

Fredrick had been drifting farther and father into the depths of the library and what he was studying. Arthur was very fearful that his father might disappear in the bowels of libraries, the source of never-ending information. This and the allure that somehow he could make spiritual contact with his dead love, would he just a step into that world and never find his way back? Or maybe even worse come to an end and discover it was just flim-flam and would give up caring. The one thought he didn't want to entertain, yet could not be avoided, was what if his father just gave up and decided to join his mother?

In the end, he and JudyAnn accepted that neither of these possibilities were anything they could control, influence, or stop his father from doing. Taking over the company's control was one of the greatest challenges he might ever face, but the understanding that he could not change his father's path would eclipse what he had first thought would be the biggest challenge.

It steadily became clear, that Fredrick was struggling to focus on anything outside of his Olivia. And this resulted in the company becoming somewhat rudderless. For almost six months, Arthur had begun exploring thoughts of initiating a competency hearing but could not bring himself to step over that cliff. While floundering, the company's financial officer and operations officer contacted him requesting a meeting with Arthur to voice their concerns.

His Father beat them to it and asked to do the same. He was waiting in the conference room when they began to arrive. Arthur did not believe he was the only one surprised that his Father had his lawyer present. He was astounded, when informed, the meeting was to begin the transfer of ownership of the company to Arthur.

The complexity of this grew to the point of taking on a life of its own. The first step in the transfer began with a one hundred and eleven page document outlining the transfer. It was just one piece of many to follow. There were reports by seven different presidents of this and that, and a incredible range of laws, needing a staff of five lawyers, international agreements, and, and…

Hans described to me how Arthur hid in his study frozen for two and a half weeks intellectually and emotionally until the silence was broken by Arthur's wife JudyAnn saying,

"Do I need to slap you, hug you, do both or just stand here until you notice me?" Arthur's freeze shattered and his emotions began melting, and sobbing took over with, "I can't, I just can't!" and the sight of his wife became blurred by the tears. Her arms wrapped him pulling him in tight to her as she cooed, "Whatever it is, together we can."

The next day began with something even worse for Arthur. Identification and distribution of all the other Folks properties was on the to do list,

"Bloody HELL, I'm not my Father, and I'm sure as hell not supposed to be the Patriarch of this damn family, that is supposed to be Robert he's the oldest! How did I agree to this BS!!" he told Hans.

For the next three days, Arthur shifted through folder after folder listing everything that his mother and father had owned. Exceptions were their personal belongings. His father already had the right to reside in the Aisling until his death, along with a substantial living allowance. What was even harder was the battle royal Arthur had in convincing his father to accept the allowance. The battle ignited when Hanson was sitting at the conference table and heard his Father exclaim,

"I don't need anything like that. I have everything I need right here in the Aisling." After shouting, pouting, and refusing, when an agreement was reached the only thing left was transcribing it into a written contract. At the end of the meeting, everybody departed except me, and Arthur who was bent over the conference table head in hands saying: "Does this nightmare ever end?" Then with head down and shoulders sagging he left for home.

That part of the nightmare didn't end for almost three more weeks. Arthur had to meet with Hanson and his brother Robert and in the process attempt to find common ground for all concerned, The stumbling block was again the true Patriarch his father, who by the way, when asked to join the meeting, refused saying,

"Do what you think is right, and I don't care what it is. I don't want to know." He then left the sitting room where they all met and returned to the library.

On the surface, it should have been Robert running what Arthur had been calling this circus except for his Father's outrage that exploded eight years earlier. Fredrick had ordered a family meeting and disclosed he was hearing rumors at the club and had followed them up with hiring a detective to investigate them. He was so agitated that he had to stand up and began pacing, with his back to them he started to speak in an uncharacteristically subdued manner, and told them,

" What was reported by this detective was that Robert is a fairy boy, a queer that liked boys. I want him out of my house and not, not, be my son." Then, without turning, Fredrick walked from the room and did not look back.

Hans with significant embarrassment continued the story by saying, "Before Robert left, my Mother hugged him with a tear slowly running down one cheek and almost in a whisper asked, "Robby, is this true? It is okay if it is, just tell me true."

"I am Mommy. I'm so sorry," he said, looking at the floor as tears fell from his eyes. He caught his breath, and between some choked back sobs and acknowledged his sexuality.

"I could not have found peace with it. I am the son of a compelling and influential family. With a father biased against anyone, as he has stated, many, many times, that are not one of us!" Robert did not believe he would ever know what exactly all this meant, but he knew it meant homosexual, Democrat, or dove. He was also sure as hell it meant people that did not speak English, have a dark complexion, and or did not support what his Father's beliefs of what the good old U.S. of A. stood for.

Arthur's hands were tied when he made decisions related to the family distribution of Mother's and Father's holdings. His father had decided to make him, in all but birth order, the "First" son, and if not for his mother's will, he would not have been allowed to provide Robert with any of the family wealth.

Olivia's will included the bequest of what they called the "Summer Home" to the oldest son Robert. It also included an operating budget, making Robert a very wealthy man, yet it would never make-up for how his Father had disowned him. Both Arthur and Hanson believed it would have been much more appropriate for Robert to inherit the Aisling estate because of his interest in the supernatural. He had been the only son sharing his mother's interest in the spiritual, and that became evident during his early childhood. This mother-son connection was also highly frowned on from his Father, yet never verbalized. Now Robert was expelled from even this shared history. It just was not to be.

To Arthur, the Aisling was just a possession, not a home, unlike in his father's eyes. Even with his transformation into an advocate of the spiritual world, Fredrick was unwilling to include Robert as family. So it was that the Aisling was to be inherited by the youngest son Hanson. This decision was justified based mostly on the magnificent library and Hanson's background as a professor and researcher.

From beginning to end, the process had taken nearly a year.

Nothing seemed finished to Arthur, even after the last papers were signed, some holdings sold, and everything distributed within his abilities. Frederick Folks, the father, favorite son of Quinn and tycoon of a shipping empire, was no more than a hermit living in the library.

It was assumed Robert resided in Europe, based on Robert's belief he could be more understood there and not treated as a subspecies. Arthur could only imagine how devastating Mother's loss was for Robert. A loss far more profound than even he could imagine.

JudyAnn and Arthur had disclosed to Hanson, after the last visit to Aisling, how they sat for hours discussing alternatives for their Father. Everything from nursing homes, committing him to a locked door facility, hospitalization, or just leaving him to roam the halls between shelves, looking for answers that could not be found. This choice was even harder as they were losing a Father that was not dead, but a ghost, roaming the shelves of the library.

One of the few times Hans had observed his brother this defeated was when he disclosed how he attempted to talk with a hunched-over specter that was his Father, yet no longer seemed present. And how futile it was when the closest to a conversation was mumbles, coughs, and rambles. Father's behavior caused almost as much sorrow for the three sons as losing their mother. She would be remembered for the comfort and total acceptance she gave to all the boys.

CHAPTER SIX

Yoyo Returning to Aisling house blind

Sounds of his car, other cars, stuff not known. BUT! not hospital sounds. Sounds are taking the place of my sight. That's not totally right, sounds and touch are taking the place of seeing.

In the hospital, but not with Owl, she learned to feel people enter her room and sounds that told her about them and what they might be doing. Some were soon-to-be forgotten smells of the hospital, and all the people working there. She always knew when Zoie or Dr. D entered the room. The tobacco he smoked had a cherry smell. Zoie smelled more like, well, more like a flower garden in early spring.

She knew Zoie and Dr. D were a couple, even without them saying so. The first time she noticed was when asking Dr. D where Zoie was, and he replied she could not visit until later. Yolanda somehow knew this, and she could smell her on him. And when Zoie came that afternoon without him, she could smell him on her. Zoie's body heat told her that she always leaned in close when she was talking. Dr. D, for the most part, never got that close. Guess it was a guy thing.

Now riding in a car and returning to Aisling House, it was all she had, smell, feel, hearing. She had not realized how much she had missed in relation to these senses. Seeing seemed to overpower them all. Now, she was just beginning to understand how vital all the senses are.

But, oh, dear God, how much she missed without seeing. Emotions were incredibly different. Anxiety, fear, and sometimes terror filled her when not in her room, especially the first few times walking outside. Even holding on to Zoie's shoulder, each step was frightening. Zoie seemed to be the only person who knew how to let her explore walking instead of telling her how.

Dr. D tried, but it was more of an attempt to control her than allowing her to practice and explore a bit more on her own. Just thinking about that difference, she began to shiver with anxiety. How in the hell is she going to learn out here!

"We are almost here," Dr. D called out from the front seat, in a way that said he wasn't sure about how to go about this process. Yolanda thought it was also Dr. D's way of handing the conversation over to Zoie. And when the sound of her voice suggested Zoie was turning toward her and then began speaking, she was sure.

"Is that what you are calling the Gatehouse?" Zoie asked in a subdued tone.

"That most assuredly is," he responded with a grin, and I plan on stopping to tell Albie and his family that we are here. I also need to invite them to join us in the next hour or so. Hans was unsure of when we would arrive so asked if I would do this. Hans would like to spend some time with us before we meet the staff. I expect everybody will want to spend time with you and Yolanda."

Yolanda was unsure what "wanting time with her meant and before she could ask, Zoie began to speak…

"Let's review some of the signals you and I discussed yesterday, mostly for my benefit, so I don't forget. Also, let me know anything else that I can be helpful with. Okay, the first is; when you would like a break from all the information or are confused about anything, just say the flowers smell nice. That will indicate you need to talk to me or need to use the Lady's room. If I respond and say, it must be my new perfume, it means I will arrange it as soon as possible. A gentle squeeze on my hand is saying something is good, right, or you agree. A firm squeeze means you do not agree, or something is wrong.

If instead, you say, I smell cherries, that will indicate that you are feeling overwhelmed, anxious, fearful, etc. I respond with, oh, that must be Damon's tobacco, meaning I will find a way to move us to a quiet space. I will stay aware of yes/no and good/bad squeezes on my hands, arms shoulders, and legs."

"We have arrived at the Gate House," Damon announced as the car came to a stop. He opened his door, stepped out and walked the flower-lined path toward the entrance. Mr. Albie Proyer, the caretaker and landscaper, came outside and greeted Damon with an enthusiastic "Welcome, Welcome, Professor Soule, come in, come in." Damon gracefully declined and suggested that he and his family come up to the Aisling at six. Albie assured Damon that they would arrive promptly at 6 o'clock. They shook hands, Damon returned to the car and continued the drive to Aisling.

Zoie and Yolanda continued to discuss their signals between verbal and physical communications. Then in mid-sentence, a loud persistent whistle erupted. Zoie, in a high pitched shout, demanded

"Is That it? I MEAN the HOUSE! For God's Sake, you must be kidding." This time, it was Yolanda who calmed Zoie and reassured her that the inside is even more impressive. Even before the statement was totally out of her mouth, she realized that wasn't a calming response to Zoie's amazement. Both she and Dr. D began, at the same time, attempting to downplay the grandeur of the Aisling. The stammering and excited comments and questions continuing to burst from Zoie clearly suggested neither Dr. D or Yolonda were close to successful.

By the time Mrs. Holbert, the housekeeper, greeted them at the door, Zoie had gotten some control of her emotions. At least enough to follow Dr. D and Mrs. Holbert to where Mr. Folks was currently awaiting them. He had heard Mrs. Holbert's greetings and had come out to welcome them. With almost a superhuman effort, Zoie attempted to maintain her composure as they entered into a room rivaling the majority of small city libraries. Thinking to herself, this was something, well somewhat like she was expecting as Damon and Yolanda both had described it. Even so, their descriptions had not done it justice.

The sound of the fire, the aroma of books, wood and leather furniture, all washed over Yolanda. This room was a place that had changed her life while helping a devastated and broken man, Mr. Folks' father. Dr. D had brought her here after Dean enlisted in the Navy and deserted her to fight in that travesty called the Vietnam war. She had been heartbroken and lost all semblance of giving a damn about most anything. She remembered very little about her arrival the first time until entering this golden world of all the books she had ever dreamed of reading and hundreds more that she had never known existed and knew she would want to read.

Today was the second time she had entered this room when she, herself, was broken and lost. She began squeezing Zoie's arm, heard a yelp, then Zoie said:

"I think I picked up a pebble in my shoe, the silly thing really hurts and please, which way to the ladies room or another room that I can, um, repair the damage." With Yolanda clutching her arm, the the two woman were directed to a lavish guest bath that also brought back memories.

As soon as they entered the room, Zoie closed the door and said,

"You are safe, here is a settee for you sit on, guiding her to it." Yolanda hesitantly reached forward with a toe, then leaned down to touch it with her fingers, turned around reached with her hand, fingertips once again making contact, she sat down with a sigh. Then burst into tears and said between sniffles and sobs…

"I can't, just can't do this. It's too damn hard. Not like in the hospital. I could hear when things were moved, and knew I needed to adjust my way around the room. Some of this was vitally important such as knowing how many steps needed to reach the restroom. If people didn't move the chair, I knew what direction and how many steps to it. Maybe, just maybe, I just should be in a hospital. I'm FUCKING BLIND!" Burying her face in her hands, she began to sob uncontrollably.

Sitting down beside her Zoie wrapped her arms around her and cuddled her as she sobbed, murmuring it's okay… I'm here don't worry… This will take a little time to get use to. We can do this together, I'm right here and not going to leave you." The two rocked back and forth, and both of them cried until a light knock on the door and, a woman's soft voice inquired, "Is everything all right. Do you need help?"

"We will be out shortly, everything is fine. It will just be a moment," Zoie called out to the unknown voice."

"Okay, Dear, I'm just here to help if I can. Oh! I am so sorry you have no idea who I am. My name is Mrs. Holbert, the housekeeper, I met you at the front entrance. I will reassure the Professor all is well, and that the two of you will return to the Library shortly. Then I will return to see if there is anything else I can do or bring to you. Unless, of course, there is something else I can do for you this moment?" After Zoie assured her all was well, Mrs. Holbert left.

Yolanda snuffed back her tears and asked for some tissues. After an unladylike nose-blowing, pushed back away from Zoie, straightened up and observed,

"She walks heavily with a limp."

"What, who?" Zoie responded, sounding somewhat startled.

"The housekeeper, Mrs. Holbert,"

"Oh! No Whoa! That proves it."

"What, what proves what?" Yolanda answered, then with a very manly nose blow, asked again,

"What?"

"You just proved that you do not, I repeat, do not belong locked away in some ridiculous hospital, especially a mental hospital cell."

"What the Hell are you talking about?" Yolanda asked, confused with a conversation neither of them seemed to understand.

"Here she comes again," Yolanda stated.

"Who is coming?" Zoie said sounding confused.

A light double tap on the door, and Mrs. Holbert asked,

"Is one of you named Dr. Philmore or Yolanda Swiftriver?"

"That is exactly what I am talking about," Zoie whispered then she answered,

"I am Dr. Philmore and Yolanda Swiftriver is with me. Can I help you?"

"Oh pardon me, Madam, I was asked to verify that it was one of you that I had spoken with earlier. The Professor was concerned if there was something amiss, due to the length of time you have been ah, occupied, Madam."

Zoie reassured Mrs. Holbert that she and Yolanda would rejoin the men shortly. She then turned back to Yolanda and with barely concealed joy asked,

"How did you know that it was the housekeeper before I heard her?"

"I don't know… I guess I just did. Just did, but you didn't. Maybe I just assumed it was her."

"Yes, But how, did you know?"

Yolanda with an edge to her voice stated,

"I just did, so what's the big deal… How did I know? I knew because… I just heard her and knew. When she walks, one foot sort of scuffs the floor, but the other one does not." A long silent pause then,

"Until right this minute, I did not know something that I did know. How can that be?"

The two of them discussed how Yolanda's hearing was beginning to compensate for the lack of her eyesight for at least another ten minutes. A stronger and more confident Yolanda took Zoie's arm and they returned to the Library.

PART FIVE

CHAPTER ONE

Damon as Aisling House Executor

As they were returning to the Library, Professor Folks was heard emphasizing strongly,

"Damon, you will not owe me a red cent, nor a pound of gratitude. It is you doing me a favor, not me doing you a favor. Yolanda brought my Father comfort when I could not, none of us could." Hearing footsteps, Hans looked toward the door, seeing the ladies, turned, and greeted them.

Damon and I were just discussing how very grateful I am that Damon and Yolanda have agreed to reside over the Aisling while my wife and I am finally taking the cruise we have promised each other for years. Pardon me, and I need to rephrase, the journey I have been promising to take with her. It is bloody time, I have neglected her far beyond any way I can repay. And you two young people are helping me follow through with my promise.

Earlier I was explaining to Damon, we also plan to take our son and daughter. It will be a family adventure long overdue. The final requirement, because of our absence, is where you become a critical part of us being able to fulfill my promise. Brother Arthur, as always, is a stickler for details. He was quite insistent I needed to appoint an executor of the Aisling estate in case of, well, in case of an unforeseen catastrophe. Guess Arthur does not entirely accept that what we are doing, is without risk. He always expects the worst.

You Damon have graciously agreed with my proposal, so the only loose end is you and Yolanda. Would you consider Aisling appropriate for your needs? Mrs. Holbert has suggested the downstairs Study is suitable for converting to your needs. Yolanda held up a hand, and Hans paused.

"Would it be asking too much if instead, that I use the same rooms as last time? The second one on the left at the top of the staircase? I think I know that area and also from there to the Library."

Hans cheerfully agreed and further suggested that the adjacent rooms would be appropriate for additional requirements such as a caregiver, and another space for any other needs. Lastly, we need a space for you, Damon, Hans continued, "I am quite sure you are not as familiar with Aisling as Yolanda, so we will have Mrs. Holbert take you on tour."

Not long after that, Damon, and Zoie were inquiring about ideas Professor Folks might have regarding identifying an appropriate caregiver when Zoie's hand went up in the air. It was like she was asking permission to speak. Her cheeks turned a bright red, and her big eyes widened with a startled expression as she began apologizing.

"I am so sorry for interrupting, but as you were talking, I think I may have come up with, I think, an ideal solution. I could assist Yolanda. Well, as best as we can, "

Just then, Mrs. Holbert announced that Mr. Albie and his family had arrived. Yolanda could see Albie in her mind. From the first time she saw him, she somehow knew she would like this man. It was his expression, one that radiated curiosity about all he saw. He would also quietly talk to things he was working on; whether, it was painting, cleaning, tending hedges, or whatever, he just seemed to care.

On the other hand, Gertie, his wife, radiated a "let me do it for you." She was the Aisling's cook in addition to Albie's helper. Gertie was much thinner then Albie probably because she never seemed to slow down, so you might say she also radiated energy. She and Albie at first could be described as polar opposites, yet they just fit together. The more Yolanda pictured the two, the more comfortable she felt being in this dream house. Fear began to subside from her shoulders to her feet. Probably the first time since meeting them again, she felt some peace.

A very soft voice said, "Do you like to be called Yolanda? Because I think I remember hearing someone calling you YoYo. I do not want to seem rude, but what would you like me to call you."

"First, I would have to know who you are and what you like to be called before I would be comfortable sharing me with you."

"My name is Maranda, Papa's daughter. "

Albie's voice broke in, and he said, "Now my girl, how might Ms. Yolanda know who you are? And how might she know you are my daughter?"

Twenty minutes later, YoYo and Maranda were best friends. By the time Maranda helped Yolanda move into, what she had referred to as YoYo's apartment, Maranda had been renamed, Randa. She was to reside in an adjoining space to be YoYo's 24/7 caregiver. Dr. D agreed to the downstairs Study. It soon became apparent that Zoie would also, most of the time anyway, be staying with him. In two days, Hans and family were scheduled to depart, or as how they referred to it as "shoving off on their adventure."

CHAPTER TWO

Developing a Lab at Aisling House

Damon felt frozen… what now? Where do I start and how? The basement, cellar, or is it just a lower level? Hans had taken him down the stairs to what he referred to as a space that might be adequate for Damon's research needs. The size was easily 20 by 30 feet in addition to other doors leading to what Hans referred to as extra spaces, that Damon could use for storage. It was beyond anything Damon had ever dreamed. The quietness alone made it perfect for restarting the study. If everything worked out, it would no longer be just a research study. Instead it had, without a doubt, evolved into a legitimate experiment in how to unlock the *in utero* experience. He now had his research laboratory and Han's had assured him that any equipment and other expenses were to be fully funded. The full realization of the actual gift Hans had granted him was brought home when Hans signed a check for $50,000. With a fatherly slap on the back and a big smile, Hans suggested he deposit it in a separate bank account just for the lab.

That was three days ago. Hans and the family's Bon Voyage party was yesterday, and with much fanfare, they had upped anchor early this morning and sailed out of the harbor. Now Damon was walking down the stairs to begin creating a layout for his new research lab. On the way, he also began musing about how Dean and Yolanda had been involved in his first attempt to use hypnosis plus regression to explore the pre-birth experiments. The two as a team were light-years past all the initial forty plus students in the regression studies.

Damon, with Dr. Folks's encouragement, began identifying the criteria and need for "highly susceptibility subjects." Damon had not included this as a qualifier when he first tested students volunteering for extra credit. As the research model developed, he had taken Dr. Folks' advice and incorporated susceptibility to hypnosis within his research design. His prior studies indicated this as the primary prerequisite for participation, yet his study design did not. Including this criterion into the design made all the difference. On the completion of the next study, he was able to identify a significantly elevated correlation. It became evident in the depth and consistency of the subjects' verbal reports and behavior patterns while in the hypnotic state. Susceptibility to the voice and environment provided was clearly a positive factor in moving the subject into deeper levels of the hypnotic trance.

Including these criteria for the subjects susceptibility led to the possibility of exploring the scientifically unexplored world of early childhood and possibly birth experiences. The findings were showing supportive data for incredible insights. It seemed that all the work Damon had put in, and all the time and information that Hans Folks had provided would provide significant dividends. They worked closely together and spent every possible moment of free time while becoming friends, vice associates, in addition to mentor and student.

The earlier studies indicated a strong positive correlation between a subject's positive score on susceptibility. Now also included an enhanced evaluation of the subject's willingness to follow suggestions from the hypnotist. Satisfied that his correlation was significant enough; they decided to co-author the finding and submit it for publication. The paper had brought both skepticism and excitement. The uncertainty was most intense within the hard science of developmental psychology. The excitement seemed to be much more aroused in the fields of parapsychology.

Hans was much more prepared for these reactions, having survived working with the government-funded programs that were still protected by the confidentiality requirements he had to sign. He could never divulge to Dean that a lot of knowledge collected in that research ended up in developing brainwashing techniques, such as training soldiers to follow commands without question. Damon decided early on that this and many other areas of Hans prior research was information he did not need to know and truthfully had no desire to know.

Both he and Hans became invested in an expanded research model that would clarify the information they were gathering. The main emphasis was to demonstrate that the research studies were based on a scientific criteria model and would stand up to a hard science scrutinization. Just at the time of their best hopes of an updated model began developing, all Hell broke loose, when Yolanda and Dean had that enormous blow-up.

The progress came to halt when the two separated in anger and despair. Yolanda became-all consumed with peace marches and demonstrations against the government and social injustice. She continued to participate in the research study but only in a half-hearted manner. Her focus seemed to flitter one moment to the next. Damon suspected her motivation was more about loyalty to him than to furthering her education. At times it seemed she was climbing a mountain trail while slogging through mud. Too Damon this appeared she was just pushing herself in order not to give up, instead of a true investment in what she was doing.

Yolanda barely completed her BS in psychology and only gained acceptance into the Master's program because of Damon's interventions and encouragement in the application process. Without him being the acting department head, he would not have been able to rescue her. Her thesis written haphazardly, her interview was at the best mediocre, and her testing had to be given an exception, that he provided. Damon had been quite aware this started talk among the faculty and was beginning to undermine his possibility for selection as the next department head. The problem was he had not found any new candidates in her league. After the continued testing a plethora of students applying for extra credit, he had only seen three, and the most promising one was at the most 49-50% of Yolanda's potential.

Hans had been contemplating retirement for close to a year before Yolanda's deterioration. He had apologized yet continued to slowly bow out of the research while he still fully and enthusiastically supported both Damon and his research. The supreme example of his support came a year and a half later when he appointed Damon, the acting Department Head, while Hans applied for and took an extended Sabbatical leave. Damon could not prove his suspicion that Hans's desire for a sabbatical leave was to allow Damon to explore and gain experience as a Department Head. Just shy of a year later, Yolanda is in the hospital, in a coma with little if any indication of regaining consciousness.

He did remember that three weeks after discovering she was in the hospital, and she still was not responding, he began to lose faith. Dr. Jameson, her primary physician, gave little assurance of when and if her prognosis would change. He said that he, his team, and a consulting psychiatrist agreed that the symptoms were not indicative of a typical coma. It was more like something halfway between a coma and the deepest level of sleep. It was somewhat like she was dreaming, yet her body was not responding to the doctors and nurses as if she were sleeping. Pinpricks, shots, being physically turned in her bed and bed baths, not one solicited a response to the monitor's brain waves. This would generally indicate a diagnosis of the patient being brain dead, yet her brain waves at times showed emotional and intellectual activity. It was like she was conscious but not in this world.

It wasn't that she was in the hospital; it was how she had come to be in the hospital. The peace outside his window had been incredibly fragile. On one terrible day, four students had died, and over a hundred were hospitalized. Most of the three hundred and twenty-two that had been arrested were now back on the campus. The exception was the seven students still in the hospital.

Changes in his world had exploded, unlike what happened to her, what was happening to the country was shocking to everyone. He had known that history suggested violence was a precursor to actual change. That Yolanda was part of that change caused him profound sadness, anger, and fear. She stood against violence, and it resulted in the violence that put her in this coma. The world was changing, things that he held as truths seemed to be slipping from his grasp. Dean's life had been at risk in Viet Nam and surely that also affected Yolonda.

Hans was facing the possibility Yolanda may not return to this world and to the research that she had inspired, even initiated he wasn't sure which. Without her, he wasn't sure where he would be today. It always seemed that each step of his life's journey directly connected to a pivotal person. Damon only knew that it was imperative his research once again had to become cutting edge and relevant. The research study, his future, and her recovery were part and parcel in his ability and opportunity to hold on to the Department Head appointment and possibly his professorship.

Even today, he could not remember when or why he went to the hospital and began sitting by her bed each day. He wasn't even sure about his motives. Was it the loss of his wife and their two children? Was it the desperation of losing the opportunity of her participation in his research? What the Hell was it? He just knew each day he went to her room and waited for her return.

Now today, this moment, he was in the basement of Aisling House, laying out a plan to resume his experimental research. Yolanda was upstairs with the possibility of restarting her participation. Dean was somewhere in the wilderness begging to return. And Zoie??

CHAPTER THREE

IT IS TIME TO RESTART

Unlike Dr. Swintnt's research that seemed a dead end, Damon's, on the other hand was going well and until recently had been surpassing any and all expectations. Until Hans returns, both he and Swintnt are the senior members of the Psychology department. Damon, as acting Department Head, will be the most visible to the department and the Chancellor. Now was the time to make a breakthrough in the experiment. If all the pieces come together, it would secure his appointment to Department Head, instead of a temporary position without benefits.

He knew research in the field of hypnotic regression was still very controversial. Before Yolanda was admitted to the hospital, Damon had begun considering the addition of adding an isolation tank designed to create a state of sensory deprivation. The design would be very similar to the design of the well-known John C. Lilly model that he had developed a little over ten years ago.

If Yolanda agrees to re-engage as a research subject, it could become the next paradigm shift in understanding personality development, formulation of thought, and even genetic-related behavior patterns. She had brought up the idea of experimenting with an isolation tank almost two years ago. He believed that she just wanted to delve into the Hippy behaviors of smoking marijuana and LSD. His own biases had prevented him from even considering the suggestion. Now would be a good time to revise his biases and advance his research to the next level.

Meanwhile, Swintnt's research was so safe it had hardly moved past his original findings. Dr. Folks taught Damon early on that grant monies and becoming published were much more critical for advancement than leading-edge research. Damon found little if any value in Swintnt's especially in a field Damon currently considered frankly as ludicrous. Considering that most grants came from governmental sources, Swintnt's study had apparently a higher potential for funding than his own. There were many restless nights Damon spent attempting to understand how Swintnt's had any value not alone government funding. With Dr. Folks' encouragement and Damons belief in his years of research a fire of hope was lit. They both knew that the regression studies one day would get the respect they deserved.

That of course has little potential, if his stays stagnant, which is not his plan. Now is the time to make a genuine difference in the world of understanding personality development. How and when beliefs are built and what the building blocks of humanism genuinely are. He believed it was imperative to bring this branch of research into respectability. To bring it out of the dark ages and prove it is a viable scientific-based research for the field of psychology.

He was very confident that he was on the cusp of this breakthrough. A project that had started six years ago now had a chance to continue to fruition with the possibility of two of the primary subjects returning. Both Dean and Yolanda had been instrumental in early research. Now that Dean had returned, it would be possible to get the two back as a team. If they helped him make the breakthrough before the Department Head appointment was made, he had a chance. If this didn't happen, then Damon knew he had better start looking for a new job. The other alternative would mean becoming submissive to all of Swintnt's mystical bullshit. Starting over was a much-preferred alternative than being his lackey.

"Well, I have over an hour before class," he thought as he left the restroom and headed back to his office. He continued thinking about

Dean and Yolanda. He hoped Dean hadn't changed too much because of Vietnam.

In his office, he checked his notes, which he seldom used during a lecture. They mostly were his preparatory exercise for lecture focus. At this moment they were also a tool to decrease his anxiety on the first day of each semester. He accepted that he was something of a showman in his teaching style, and his appearance was just another method to gain the student's attention. A trait he was quite sure came directly from his mother.

Damon received his first name due to a whim of his mother's. His parents had received the joyous news of his impending birth in their thirties. His father was thirty-nine, and she was thirty-five. According to their stories, he had heard most of his life, the first words from his Mother's on hearing the news, was "Damn his soul." At the time, he was sure the reference had been toward his father.

As the story goes, the first time his mother had heard she was pregnant, her doctor had somewhat cautiously made the announcement that she was pregnant. Angela Soule had not been known for her "let's have a baby" attitude. She had an extremely active lifestyle in both social and intellectual endeavors. The two in her mind were never competing as the primary in importance, instead she believed they balanced each other.

The arrival of a "blessed event" was, to say the least, an inconvenience. It wasn't until her seventh month of pregnancy that she began to accept the concept of motherhood. This acceptance arrived at the same time she was sure her baby would be a boy. Angela did not know how she knew this; she just knew. Thus as the story is told, Angela felt the name Damon Soule had a touch of poetic justice, along with a feel of power and mystery.

Damon had lived up to both his name and heritage. He had been a comfortable child to raise, quiet, intense, and yet social. Even as a child, Damon had a presence. Radiating a strength of purpose in most everything he did, yet the things he did always seemed slightly off-center.

Dogs, cats, and other pets were nice, but for Damon, a fish tank was much more enjoyable. At four years old, he began to refer to the family's twenty-gallon aquarium as the fish world. He watched the fish and began to make up stories about their social lives in their fish world. When Damon's father, Nigel, would clean the tank, Damon always had well thought out ideas of how their society needed to be designed. At first, Nigel went along, thinking his son's ideas would be silly, but by the third suggestion, it became clear Damon was creative, and his plans for this miniature world made sense.

When Damon started school, he came home the second day, very quiet and apparently upset. Angela asked him how he had enjoyed school. His reply was, "When do I get to learn something?" It wasn't until graduate school he began to feel intellectually challenged. He had finally found a subject that was complex enough to excite him. Most of all he was intrigued class, after class by human behavior, specifically what caused it. Were humans born with predetermined behavior patterns versus how much did we learn? Now that was truly challenging. His interest and excitement continued to build until it became a life passion. He found a world that told him stories instead of him telling stories about it.

His passion for understanding human behavior had received national recognition in both academia and the lay world. The crow jewel was developing techniques utilizing hypnosis combined with a meditation trance for deep therapy, (*ie. train people in deep meditation, combined with hypnosis*). This was the basis of his doctoral thesis. Because of rigid adherence to scientific principals, his research was not only respected; it was also published.

Damon found himself disappointed when this recognition did not translate into many job offers from highly respected universities. All his life, he had risen to the top of all his endeavors. Now he had to learn a new lesson… humility. His type of research appeared to be too radical for all but a few of the lesser-known universities. Only one of these appeared to be interested in more than the recognition that his research had received, and seemed interested in the actual research.

He accepted an associate professorship in psychology at the Marigold University, a small quiet campus outside of the San Francisco Bay area. The school itself reflected a place of tranquility. Brick buildings nestled in lush foliage, winding paths, benches scattered, and students were walking, studying, and deep in discussion. As he strolled the campus for the first time, laughter, chatter, and words of strong commitment floated around him. Even the university's nickname Maggie U reinforced his feelings of being in a daydream or painting of the perfect Mom and apple pie idea of what higher education was supposed to look like.

These feelings stayed with him until things started unravelling. The positive results of his research had begun to slow down for almost four years. It was now to the point that the findings were less than significant. He needed or at least hoped the return of Dean would stimulate the research and help settle Yolanda. First things first, and which would come first?

CHAPTER FOUR

Driving to Tempest Cove

Dean's head was buzzing as he was driving back to civilization. Dr. D. had not elaborated on what had changed. Instead he had just said Yolonda was ready to see him. Now he and someone named Zoie had liberated her from the hospital. Gave him directions to a place called Aisling House and said Albie the caretaker was notified that Dean would be arriving.

The most significant buzz was how long it had been since seeing Yolonda. Dean slowed the Corvette and stared at the massive three-story home named Aisling House. When it first came into view, he had a twinge of discomfort. He wasn't sure how much Yoyo had changed, but if this house was any indication, he was in for some surprises. Psychic phenomenon and this house sure seemed to fit each other. If this was where Yoyo's field of research lead her, he had to admit the setting was perfect.

He liked the way the house sat overlooking the ocean and how it was surrounded by forest. Yet the feel was spooky, and truthfully the house was downright ugly. It had to be ancient as if placed here from some old horror movie filmed in the Deep South. If it had not been brick, Dean was sure it would have crumbled before his parents got out of diapers. The unknown of seeing Yoyo had welled up inside of him. Last time he had felt this way with belly butterflies fluttering was his first time taxiing onto an aircraft carrier catapult. He just hoped seeing her again would be less traumatic than having a catapult kick him in the ass. Long repressed memories of that final explosion between Yoyo and himself had come flooding back as he climbed from the car and started up the long walkway.

Dean stood in front of the oversized doors and stared at the door clapper. Good God, he thought, it even has a medieval style door knocker. With sweaty hands and adrenalin flowing, he reached for the clapper. Four thudding raps with the clapper didn't result in the door opening. Surely she couldn't have forgotten I was coming, he thought, feeling tiredness wash over his body. Damn it! He had been driving for six hours. That speeding ticket, hopefully, is for something more than a quick drive up the coast. He knocked again.

He tried the door, thinking that she may not be able to hear the clanging. It swung inward as if protesting. That might be due to its size, he thought, stepping into an entrance room of magnificent proportions. This place had to be even bigger than it looked from the outside. How in the hell was she able to afford such a place? Dr. D had not prepared him for this level of luxury. The size was utterly overpowering.

An elegant yet massive staircase emptied into the room. If anything, it just magnified the hugeness that stretched before Dean. His feet made hollow echoes as he walked toward the far end of the room. An open door, the only open door, waited, lights flicked through the opening. Just as he stepped through it something bounced off his leg and disappeared behind a big leather chair. He had choked down a scream, just a little one, and maybe even dribbled a little pee into his shorts. He decided it could only be a huge cat or perhaps a dog.

Little fingers of ice crawled up his spine. He was not sure what this place was about, but Dr. D. sure as hell did not tell him it was a place out of a horror movie. Something just did not feel right; a Vietnam Veteran like himself to feel like this didn't make sense. He had a chest full of medals, and here he was acting like a bit player in a monster movie. Walking farther into a room that must be over twenty feet deep, he was trying to convince himself YoYo may have fallen asleep while waiting for him, instead of being the guest of Frankenstein.

Again his spine iced up as creepy fingers seemed to crawl around his back. Then he saw her, well kind of, no he was sure it was. It was YoYo sitting in front of a fireplace fitting the size of the room, but the flickering light was not coming from it. Long lit candles scattered around the room, and evidence they had been burning a long time. When he called her name, she did not move. The room seemed to be sucking the heat from his body, yet the closer he walked toward the fireplace, the warmer the room felt. A large pile of burnt embers with some dim red coals glowing here and there with one small flame and a trail of smoke rising. Testimony to a not so long ago fire. The embers and coals did not seem capable of providing the heat he was feeling. If he didn't know better, he would think the fireplace was sucking the heat from the room, instead of heating it.

Mustiness seemed to be drifting through the smell of leather, candles, incense, and long-dead wood fires. YoYo still hadn't moved or looked up, even when he repeatedly called her name. Scenes of old whodunit's came back as he reached for her shoulder, but instead of falling forward with a knife in her back, she just turned to stare blankly at him, looking like somebody that recently escaped from a wax museum.

As his stomach started playing partners with his spine, she blinked, and without looking around, smiled and said, "Hello Dean," as if she were opening the front door. Then she turned around, her cheeks and eyes took on the embarrassed look he remembered so well. The look made him want to reach out for her, yet he still wasn't sure where they stood. She was still the most beautiful woman he had ever met, and the years seemed to have just increased her beauty.

She stood up with tears of joy and started walking toward him as if she were able to see, and then she hugged him. It was just like a dream that may have helped him survive all the years of war if only they had not broken up.

"Oh, I'm so sorry, I must have dozed off in front of the fireplace," she exclaimed, as her head moved in a manner suggesting she was looking toward the fireplace. Then her lips were on his. The fireplace and chill of the room soon forgotten. So were the years that had passed since the fight.

"Let me show you my little hide-a-way," she said with the little wrinkles around her eyes coming out, the way they always did when she was feeling mischievous. Dean was getting the creepy feelings back… running up his neck, how could she look and behave so normal without being able to see? Tearing his eyes away from her, he began really looking at his surroundings for the first time. The room they were in was a very well-stocked library. The craftsmanship that built the floor to ceiling bookshelves was incredible. Everywhere he looked, there was the same level of attention to detail. With her standing beside him and taking such distinct pleasure in having the opportunity to continue her studies, in as she put it "this magnificent relic," he started feeling pretty damn foolish about the icy spine routine.

Here she was living in this house all by herself and he was getting spooked. He wondered what she would think if she knew? Instead, he attempted to shake off the chills and replace them with the warmth she was displaying. Then she said,

"Hey! Remember me? After not seeing me for over all those years, what do you think?"

Dean's mouth engaged way before his brain as he heard himself say,

"You aren't acting like you're, ah, ah blind?"

"I guess Dr. D left out some of the minor details, Huh!" She stated with her face turning away and changing from smiles to something between anger, or maybe embarrassment. Dean was not sure what it was, but he started to stammer an apology. All YoYo said, walking toward a couch was, "We need to sit down so I can fill you in, I had assumed that he told you the whole story, but I guess not."

She began in a somewhat monotone to describe the demonstrations and the violence that ensued against the kids that were protesting and then regaining consciousness in a hospital bed, not knowing what had happened or how long she had been in a coma. Tears were forming at the corner of her eyes as she continued the horror story. Her voice began to change to a more robust timber as each sentence increased in strength, it was like she was trying to strong-arm the tears away.

Dean stood up, gently moving to the couch where she was sitting. He slowly sat down and began scooting closer. She continued as if unaware of his changed position, still explaining how hard it had been, first to believe that she was no longer able to see, then the fear of trying to find her way in this new invisible black environment.

That was when tears began to flood her cheeks, and Dean reached out to embrace her. She turned towards him, clutched him to her in a desperate way, and began to sob, choke, cough, and fight to catch her breath. The intensity of her emotions touched inside of him, and his tears began to fall. They sat holding each other for a length of time that he could not gauge. It felt like forever, yet seemed to have just begun.

He pulled her to him and just sat there, savoring the feel of her. He finally choked out the words, "God, I've missed you," he murmured as their lips merged into one. After a very long moment, the unknowns of each other invaded the comfort of being together again. She pulled back and nudged him to move back a little so she could continue.

Hours passed with little awareness as she described the doctors, psychologist, psychiatrist, and so many other experts and professionals that were supposedly there to help. Instead, she felt prodded, pushed, pricked, and shoved around. Everyone seemed to demand her to be on their schedules. Also, they expected her to accept their beliefs about what was best for her.

"And that wasn't the worst part," she said, "It was the part when nobody seemed to agree with anybody else. They added physical therapy saying it was needed as a result of my long-term comma. It was like people were materializing next to me wanting this and that. I did not have a moment to even think, well, not when I was awake. I was living in nonstop commotion not only in my mind, but even outside my room. There was nowhere to hide except for going deeper inside my mind to escape from all of it.

Imagine," she told him "if you had days, weeks, and then months of nurse's aides, nurses, doctors, physical therapists, neurologists, sociologists, psychologists, and even social workers coming up with diagnoses, treatments, and new referrals all explained in Medicalease.

My brain is broken. I cannot see nor be pressured to follow all of these people in how to fix me! Please don't get me wrong; these same professionals were the ones that saved my life, took care of me in a coma, and did not know if I would ever gain consciousness again. They saved my life, I'll always be owing them a debt that I can never pay, but the aftermath was horrible. At times I just wanted to go back far away. Not into the coma but just to someplace that was safe and caring, not medical caring, human caring.

I know I'm not making a lot of sense, but it was just what it was, It wasn't until Doctor D. introduced me to Zoie, well I should call her Dr. Philmore, but she prefers me to call her Zoie, so I will. She is both a Psychologist and an MSW. She was the one that started, with Dr. D's help also, to back the buzzards away. Both she and Dr. D suggested I needed to start moving toward independent living, so I could start living my life and not entertain a hospital full of professionals."

Dean was struggling to keep up with all the twists and turns that YoYo had clearly gone through and continued to be confused about how she came to reside in Aisling House. Luckily a young woman, he guessed somewhere between 17 and 19, came into the room and with a cheery voice announced it was time to eat.

A bright smile animated YoYo's face, and then she introduced Maranda; according to YoYo, she was her own Anne Sullivan. This was stated so profoundly that Dean had to break in and ask who this Anne Sullivan was.

"She was the lady that helped Hellen Keller, and you do know who that is," YoYo asked with curiosity. Dean admitted he had heard of her, but didn't know much.

"She was someone that totally changed how we thought about blindness," Yolanda said while continuing to enthusiastically educate Dean about how Hellen was not only blind but also deaf. How she had written books, gained a college degree, and even starred in a movie, and that it was Anne Sullivan that made all that possible.

Far into the night, the two remained on the couch, exploring the past. Dean's participation tended toward being supportive and understanding. He knew this was the time to listen and his chance to share later. There seemed to be some similarities between both his and her experience during the last six years that he could share later. Right now, he was just content to sit close with shoulders and thighs touching as she described the Aisling, Zoie, and the incredible honor that Professor Hans and his family had bestowed on her.

Her focus remained on the house. And how Dr. D finally persuaded her to at least come and meet the people invested in her and also helping her to navigate her new environment. Toward early morning, YoYo with her head nestled in his lap, they both fell asleep.

CHAPTER FIVE

Many Levels of Seeing

This is Incredible! Yo... Dang, Lon. What the... I am seeing! I'm with Owl flying close to the clouds. Now beginning to glide downward. The sun's red, yellow, white rays starting to light the east as Owl glides closer and closer to the ground.

In the lodge of She-Elder Womb Wise, across the embers sitting on robes listening. She-Elder said Owl was her spirit guide, not her eyes. Dances wants to argue, respect would not be shown. Dances remains quiet. Her job is to hear not to argue. She-Elder is saying,

"Dances-as-Rain sees, not Owl. I see questions in your eyes that say do not see. What are your questions?"

"If I am blind, in, in the other world, how is it I see here and not through Owl's eyes, She-Elder?"

"Little Sister, do you not see when in the dream world?"

"But She-Elder that is in a dream, not in real life."

"If you do not see, then what is it in your dream?"

"That is not the same. I am blind in the other land. That is what I mean by not seeing."

She-Elder was silent for many breaths before resuming,

"When you do not see with your eyes, do you see inside your head?"

Both women were silent, studying the embers. Finally, Dances tossed her head, tears of frustration trickling down both cheeks, and said,

"I do not understand. I want to, but I don't. Please tell me what you mean, please."

"Your Warrior has returned, what color are his eyes?"

"They are gray. When pleased they lighten and when passionate they darken."

"So you see his face?"

"No, no, I remember his face."

"So, can you close your eyes and see his eyes?"

"Yes but, I…"

"Little Sister buts are what we sit on. They are not what we speak. Can you see him in your mind's eye?"

"Yes, bu,"

"So you do see. You see me here, at this place, at this time. Is it possible that how we see might be different from what you are use to calling seeing?"

Their talk lasted until after the red embers turned dark, and the sun began to hide behind the mountains. When it was entirely hidden, Yolanda awoke with a kink in her neck, and Dean was quietly snoring with his head leaning over to one side. She wanted to reach up and touch him, yet at the same time did not want to awaken him. Slowly she reached up and over very slowly until her hand brushed his hair. Feeling around gently, it was apparent if not for the sofa's arm, she was sure he would have fallen over the side, possibly on to the floor.

Moving ever so slowly, she wormed her way out from one of his arms and was able to sit upright. She stood up and quietly climbed the stairs to her rooms, sat down on the toilet and began replaying She-Elder's message about seeing. The first thought coming to mind was why she came all the way upstairs instead of the restroom off of the Library? The only answer coming to her was so he would not see. See that I entered into a bathroom? Really?

Finishing her business, she washed her hands. Then she went to her desk and faced toward the window in front of her. The words see and seeing floating through her thoughts. It could not have been the seeing She-Elder was asking about. Sure of that and feeling very silly in even thinking such a thing, Yolanda returned to the restroom to shower and freshen up, she did not want Dean to see her like this.

A light tapping on her room door and the sound of Dr. D's voice asking if she was awake, began the rest of the day. Twenty minutes later, she joined Dr. D, Zoie, and according to Randa, a very rumpled looking, yet ever so very handsome looking young man. Yolanda, with all that had happened, and last evening filling her thoughts had apparently not informed Randa of Dean's arrival. Yesterday had been her day off, and she had come to Yolanda's rooms a few minutes after Dr. D's knock on her door.

All in a whirl, Yolanda had left Randa, and you could say, in the dark. She chuckled, wanting to share her "In the Dark" joke with her later when they had some private time. After somewhat of a late breakfast, Zoie and Dr. D made their excuses and departed. As they were leaving, Dr. D requested that he would very much enjoy having Dean spend tomorrow with him for some catch up time. Randa, after Yolanda had updated her, also found several errands that needed to be tended too. Yolanda and Dean had the rest of the day to themselves.

CHAPTER SIX

Dean Shares His Seeing

They both skirted their breakup and instead spent the day talking. Mostly about Aisling, Professor Folks, Zoie, and the research project, Dr. D set up in the basement. YoYo became highly animated in both her face and verbalization, especially when she began describing what Dr. D was developing as the next step in the regression studies. How his thoughts of using some new experimental ideas for exploring avenues to increase her pre-birth memories. The importance of Zoie and Dr.D working as a team yet exploring separate directions. Yolanda's excitement about Zoie's current focus that was exploring how several new techniques may be useful in treating both Yolanda's PTSD and even a possibility of her blindness.

Dean was listening, sort of, yet caught himself losing focus on her words. He found himself studying her more than listening to her. Most of the time, he forgot her blindness. Watching her increased his fascination with the ways YoYo navigated her environment. Even now, as she was talking, it seemed as if she was looking around. Other times she seemed to be looking into his eyes. He had not observed her bumping into, reaching out with her hands for guidance, nor showing any confusion as to where she was in the room.

"Did I lose you? It seems you are not here, you know, with what I am telling you."

His focus snapped back to her words, her face and eyes staring into his. How in the bloody hell does she do that, he thought. Then he said,

"Not at all, I am absolutely interested, actually more fascinated than you could ever know."

"Well, alright, then, what do you think about Dr. D's idea of including sensory deprivation in his research study?"

"I am at a loss. I just need more information. All this is new to me. Guess I am more interested in your thoughts and how you feel about actually getting into the Tank thing he is setting up." With some relief, he began to listen to her. Instead of the thoughts in his head as she returned to the subject matter.

She began describing how she had been the one to educate Dr. D about the experiments Timothy Leary and others were doing. With psychedelic substances such as psilocybin mushrooms, mescaline, and something else called LSD. All of them, she told him, were said to create what she referred to as a "transcendental" experience.

"If you did the educating, are you also suggesting that you were doing some of that stuff?"

"I haven't told Zoie and Dr. D that I was smoking some weed, but I think Zoie might suspect."

"What were you smoking?" Dean broke in, "What the hell is that?"

"You know, pot, marijuana, everybody was doing it. Let me rephrase that, college kids, some professors, a lot of people were doing it."

"What the hell, that stuff is bad! And against the law! What were you thinking? Is that why the National Guard attacked you and the others?"

Just as Yolanda was starting to retort hotly, Mrs. Holbert stepped into the room and announced lunch. She led them to the west patio table. Dean continued to observe YoYo as they were seated. He knew she was blind, but boy, he was hard-pressed to identify anything indicating her blindness. When she began sitting down on the patio chairs, her body language suggested she could see Mrs. Hobert, even behaving as if she was looking directly at her face while saying,

"Come on have a seat, Mrs Hobert is a very, very excellent cook."

Once he was seated, she placed her napkin on her lap, picked up her spoon, and dipped a spoon full of savory chowder. Bringing it up toward her lips, apparently inhaling the aroma and placed it in her mouth. Dean could not take his eyes away, studying for any indication she was unable to see the food in front of her. When she reached for a slice of bread, he began to reach out to help her. Their hands touched, she hesitated then when he pulled his hand back she asked,

"You may have this piece if you would like, and picked it up from the plate and moved it slightly forward in his direction."

With an incredulous tone to his voice, he asked, "How did you do that?"

"Do what?"

"It was like you can see. First, it was your chowder. You even knew where to locate the bread. Most of all, knowing where to and how to offer the bread to me. Not only that, but you also walk around this place and do other things that I would swear you need full vision to do."

A long pause suggested she was unsure what to say, a facial expression indicating something like fear or maybe embarrassment then almost in a whisper said,

"Sometimes, I can. Not like you think, just," continuing with verbal circles around the topic yet not adding to it.

With encouragement and some cajoling from him, she resumed describing what happened during the time she was in an unconscious state,

"I was flying above the trees. There were people below and a campfire. And I landed on a tree branch, and I know you might laugh or think I'm, well, you know, a little loony. But it was real, and I mean really, real. I was looking through the eyes of an owl." She turned her head away in a gesture, clearly indicating an "I can't look at you," behavior.

Dean struggled to find an appropriate response, and when a tear began forming on the corner of her eye he resumed with,

"When I was camping in the woods up north, I met a Crow."

"What do you mean, you met a crow. You mean a bird, a crow?"

"I'm not sure I met him, or he was the one that met me. I was lost, and ahead of me was a big ugly crow. It was on a path leading off in a direction I was not considering. It began cawing, initially, I just thought it was some dumb bird. I kept ignoring it, it kept cawing, and I kept walking toward a different trail than it was on. When I refused to follow it and turned the other way, it, well, he, it, well it shit on my head. I lost my mind. I mean, I went insane and started chasing the damn thing. It would just do a hop, flap, and be totally out of reach."

"So what happened?" she managed to ask through her laughter.

"I ran out of breath, started laughing, and before I knew it, I was laughing so hard I sat down in the middle of the path. When I looked up, it was… oh, maybe fifteen or twenty feet farther down the trail, standing in the middle looking at me with one big ugly eye cocked toward me. I swear it was just waiting, waiting for me to follow him. So I did, and the big ugly ass bird somehow knew I was lost and led me back to where I was camping. One hop, one flap at a time."

"Bull, you made that up just to make me feel less silly about being an owl, now isn't that right?" He denied, she smiled and did not believe him, and the two of them talked until the sun began to fall below the horizon. Dean was just starting to ask if she wanted to go inside because it was getting dark. As he began to speak, YoYo reached out and asked if he would like to go in because it was getting dark. Taking her hand and showing his bewilderedment by saying,

"How in the hell, did you know that? You are blind?"

With a chuckle, she quietly said,

"Maybe, maybe not, maybe owl is here. If you would kindly follow me, we will ask if Mrs. Holbert has something to snack on until dinner is prepared." Dean continued to be astounded by YoYo's ability to navigate through the many rooms, know that it's getting dark, and so many other seeing things. And the Owl thing she was not very clear about that.

During that night, he tossed and turned until he got out of bed. Somewhere around midnight or so, he wandered down to the library.

Maybe a book or magazine article would help decelerate his racing mind. The moon was shining bright, as he stared out the glass doors that opened out to the patio, where the two of them had been sitting earlier in the day. Walking up to the doors, he became fixated on the beauty outside. The view was reminiscent of silver artwork. Only this view was a full, life sculpture. A vista that a person like himself could only dream of not alone be part of.

That's when an owl hooted and a caw followed. Then something touched Dean's shoulder. He was sure if he hadn't peed in his jockeys, he sure as hell dribbled in them. A whispering voice said,

"It is just me wandering around in the dark."

"What in the hell?" his quivering voice demanded to the sweet smiling face of YoYo.

"Didn't mean to scare you," she replied with an even more full smile. Feeling his cheeks beginning to flush with embarrassment, all Dean could say was,

"You might think to announce yourself instead of sneaking up on someone like that. I did not see you come in," his voice trailed off as he watched that incredible smile widen even more.

"I think I see what you mean," she said as she began to laugh. Before Dean was even aware of it, he joined in until they were laughing to the point tears were forming. It was how she had emphasized the word see.

As the two lovers fell asleep in each other's arms, dreaming of their new future together. A crow cawed, and a screech owl replied.

I invite you to explore the continuing story of Yolanda, Dean and company in 'What Reality?' available in early 2021.- C. R. Couron

www.ingramcontent.com/pod-product-compliance
Lightning Source LLC
Chambersburg PA
CBHW070951190726
48292CB00004B/1420